ANDERSON PUE
ANDERSON

HOW TO S A V E

A *Life*

AMBER NATION

HOW TO SAVE A *Life*

Cover and Formatting by Shoutlines Design
Editing by Anna Coy of AGC Editing

I dedicate this book to a group of fabulous, kickass women, in which I am so blessed to be able to call my friends,

The IndiePendents

Annalisa, Delisa, Tara, Ashley, Alissa, Kay, Casey, Cassy, Savannah, Ashley, and Rachael. Each and every one of you mean the world to me. Spork friends for life!

ACKNOWLEDGEMENTS

First and foremost the three people who mean the most to me in life: My husband **Jarrod** and my girls, **Alexis and Olivia**: Thank you for being my constant support system and encouraging me every single step of the way. I would've never ever started this journey if it weren't for the three of you.

My besties: My cousin and BFF **Melanie Brock**, my fellow Neon Trees fanatic **Amanda Evenson**, my author twin **Annalisa Nicole**, and my Facebook BFF **Delisa Lynn**, thank you for always being there for me. I am so glad that I can always count on the four of you. Near or far, no matter the distance, no matter if I haven't met you in person yet, I love each one of you more than words can even express.

The IndiePendents: What can I say that hasn't already been said? It's so nice to be in such a tightknit group of ladies who can answer your questions within a moment's notice. I hope I have the opportunity to meet each and every single one of you, or even to get us all in the same place at the same time. That would be one hell of a good time!

Nation Fixation: You ladies are a fabulous group of supporters and I greatly appreciate all of your help with trying to get my name and my books out into the world of reading! I love you all!

My betas: **Chelsie Leverette, Chrystal Nation, Keesha McCallum, Melanie Brock, Ashley Volk, Delisa Lynn, Tracy Brewer, Ashley Ragsdale, Ashley Hampton, and Crissy Sutcliffe**: Thank you so much for taking the time out to read and review *How To Save A Life* before it was released and for making sure that it was the best it could possibly be! I greatly appreciate your time and your support!

The two people that without them, this book would've never been possible. **My cover designer and formatter Rachel Mizer with Shoutlines Design**: You've done it again, created a masterpiece out of FIVE different photos! I cannot wait to work with you again to see what you will come up with next! I greatly appreciate our talks and your awesome creative mind! And my editor **Anna Coy**: What can I say that hasn't already been said? You are absolutely amazing and have a great eye for editing! I am so thankful that I was introduced to you and can't wait to continue to work with you!

Enticing Journey Book Promotions - Ena and Jennifer: Thank you again for organizing everything from the cover reveal, to release day promotions, and the blog tour! I greatly appreciate all of the hard work you do for us authors!

And last BUT certainly not least - **The Readers, Reviewers, and Bloggers**: THANK YOU from the bottom of my heart for the constant outpouring of support and encouragement! I appreciate it more than you will ever know! I love each and every single one of you!!!

Prologue

4 Years Ago

Mike

Little did I know, that one single, solitary phone call would change the course of my entire life, alter my outlook on the world, and how I perceived things. I wanted to disengage myself from everyday mundane activities to just wallow in my self-infused misery. To let the guilt consume me.

Why did it have to happen?

The day started off as any other normal Monday morning. I was awoken by the tiny little human that thought it was hilarious to act like a monkey and climb up on the end of her mother's and my bed. The light from the hallway filtered in as she shoved open the bedroom door, and I heard the patter of her feet as she ran across the floor. I could just picture her placing her little size eight foot on the first spindle of our footboard and hoisting herself onto the mattress, then having to push her mass of curly ringlets out of her face with her pudgy, little hand. Giggles ensued as she crawled up in between my wife's and my resting, prone form. I had to feign sleep, because if she didn't get to do this next part, it would result in tears. But not just any tears, alligator tears, the ones that could turn on and off like a switch, it was just better not to deal with an enormous meltdown.

Inching her way up towards my face, I waited for when she would take those little hands, smash my cheeks together and smack a big sloppy good morning kiss on my lips, and then a massive tickle fight would take place. It was our morning routine, one that she looked forward to every morning. Ok in all seriousness, I did as well. She thought it was the best thing being able to wake up daddy in the mornings.

Right before she got to the best part, Erin, my wife had to

spoil our fun. "Hannah would you stop it already?" she screamed at our precious three year old daughter, which had her halting in place.

Throwing the blankets off of my body, I sat up in bed to at least get my good morning hug from my little princess.

Grasping her tightly in my embrace, I gave her a kiss atop of her strawberry blonde hair, a color she inherited from her mother. Those beautiful baby blues looked up at me with unshed tears gathering in the creases of her eyes. "It's ok princess. Why don't you go potty and put your clothes on that we picked out last night, yeah?" I said lightly, trying to diffuse the situation, and get her mind off of it before the meltdown occurred. She smiled so brightly, it revealed the little gap in between her baby teeth and shook her head up and down.

I helped her off the bed, and she ran off to get dressed and ready for school. Scrubbing my fingers in my unkempt hair, I turned to look at my wife, who had turned on her side away from me and obviously went back to sleep. I sighed wondering if and when things would ever get better between the two of us. We were high school sweethearts, but I've felt us drift apart for quite some time now.

I normally took Hannah to preschool on my way to work, but today it would be different. I had to go into work early to open up my father's mechanic shop, since he had to take my ma to a doctor's appointment, first thing this morning.

I was the head mechanic for Jameson Auto, owned by my father Michael Jameson Sr. so it was my responsibility to step up to the plate. Jameson Auto was the most reputable auto mechanic in Wentzville, a suburb just outside of St. Louis.

I enjoyed working with my father, some people didn't have the luxury of saying that. But my parents were amazing people, and I honestly couldn't see working anywhere else. Erin wasn't too thrilled being married to an auto mechanic, but when it was in your blood and you enjoyed doing it, you went with it. I began tinkering with cars at an extremely young age, taking apart my bicycles and putting them back together again.

When I was sixteen, my father bought me basically a shell of a 1966 Ford Mustang; you thought I'd hit the lottery. I was ecstatic to be able to build my first car from the ground up. Dad and I would spend our weekends rummaging through the salvage yards, looking for parts to use for my car. It fascinated me how mechanical things worked, so it was also a learning experience as well as bonding between father and son. We continuously worked on it until it was in prime condition, well for a totally restored muscle car. It was painted a cherry red, and you could see your reflection in the hood whenever she was freshly washed and waxed. I was going to keep that car forever, until it ran to the ground, then I would rebuild it all over again.

I was able to keep my Mustang for six glorious years, until I heard the words, 'I'm pregnant.' I sold my old favorite girl so I could be a daddy to my new favorite princess. I still miss that car to this day, but it was a sacrifice that I didn't resent or regret making. I would always make sure Hannah had the world, she would always come first to anything and anyone, including Erin.

After having Hannah, Erin suffered major depression. At first it was just a mild case of postpartum depression, but within a few weeks it escalated to full blown and out of control. Things would get better whenever she took her medicine, but when she didn't, I often came home to a messy house and Hannah screaming her head off while in her swing, or forgotten food on the stove. It took me threatening divorce and taking Hannah away for her to finally get help and stick to her medication regimen.

But things didn't stay better for very long. I would work forty to fifty hours a week at the garage, and come home having to pick up the house, catch up on laundry and make dinner, you name it, I did it. Erin was home all day long and didn't see the need in accomplishing chores that she knew I would do. I wasn't your average twenty-two year old, I had more responsibility than most. While it didn't bother me taking care of Hannah, I felt like our relationship was merely one-sided, my side being weighed down so heavily, at any moment the stress of it all would break me.

I was under the impression, that this whole marriage thing meant dual and equal partnership, but I could've been very wrong. I knew that's what it meant to me. Hannah and I honestly would've been better off by ourselves.

Then Hannah turned three and was eligible for preschool. Erin stood by her theory that Hannah needed to go to interact with other children her age and I agreed. So three days a week, I brought Hannah to school on my way into work, and picked her up on my lunch hour and brought her home, while Erin did, whatever Erin did. I couldn't tell you what she spent her time doing during the day and I guess I'll never know.

Finally, getting out of bed, I went into our walk-in closet and dressed in my standard uniform of blue jeans that had seen better days, no matter how many times they've been washed you could never really rid them of the grease stains, and a navy blue t-shirt that had Jameson Auto stitched in white lettering on the pocket. Grabbing my dingy work boots, I sat on the bed to slip them on and lace them up.

Erin was still lying there, so I nudged her shoulder, "Erin, you need to get up and get ready, you have to take Hannah to school." If she didn't get a move on, Hannah would end up missing Weekend Review, her favorite part of a Monday morning at school.

Rolling over and letting out a groan was her way of letting me know that she was irritated, "Why can't you take Hannah?" she whined.

"Because I have to open the shop. Dad has to take Ma to the Doctor. I told you this once on Friday and twice yesterday." I reminded her numerous times, because I knew it would come down to this, it always did.

"I don't know why your mom just can't drive herself, she shouldn't be so lazy."

Feeling my blood begin to boil, I released a deep sigh, there was no use getting into this with her right now, even though she was the one being lazy. I didn't have the time, and I was already worried about my ma's appointment and how everything was going to pan out. "Erin, she isn't lazy, they are going to find out the results from her biopsy. They found a lump in her breast, remember? I think that constitutes both of them going and me opening up the shop for them don't you?" I didn't even hang around to listen for her response, it probably would've pissed me off further.

Getting Hannah's breakfast situated, I poured my coffee

out of the pot and into a travel mug. Black with two sugars, just the way I liked it. Erin finally made her appearance as I was heading out the door, I looked up at her to see her ignoring me, so I went to Hannah and gave her our signature goodbye, an Eskimo kiss, where we rubbed our noses together. It made her giggle every, single time.

"Bye, princess, you have a good day." I said while looking into those crystal baby blues.

Putting on another glorious grin, which always tugged at my heartstrings, she spoke in her little melodic voice, "Bye, Daddy. I love you!"

"I love you too, princess."

It was pushing past lunchtime, and I hadn't heard from my dad about my ma's appointment, being anxious was the name of the game. My mother had located a small mass in her breast about a month or so ago, so she had been going to various appointments to get mammograms, ultrasounds, and lastly, a biopsy. Today was the results of the biopsy and my mom was beside herself with worry.

My dad was also worried, but he hid it well. I could see the underlying tension in his body, and he just hadn't been his usual self these past few weeks, the stress was starting to take its toll on him. My father was her rock, her knight in shining armor, she could lean on him for anything and he would always reassure her that everything would be ok. Taking things one step at a time and day by day, that's all anyone could do. I envied the relationship they had, even after thirty years of marriage, they acted like two love crazed teenagers.

I was worried as well, but I had to be strong, and I had to be there for my father to lean on when he finally cracked. I had never seen my father shed a single tear or ever let worry or stress get the best of him, but I knew his time was coming. No one could let all of that fester within yourself without ultimately bursting at one point or another.

And the fact that Erin didn't show one ounce of sympathy, just proved how ill-fitted we were for each other. Everything was always about Erin. I even had to take a break from fixing an air conditioner to make sure she still remembered to pick up Hannah. She was sleeping when I called, but at least I could take worrying about Hannah getting picked up from school off of my list now. I needed to have a sit down talk with Erin and see where she thought our relationship was headed, I couldn't deal being in a one-sided, loveless marriage for much longer; Hannah needed better stability in her life.

I went back to work, fixing the stubborn air conditioner in a car that had seen the inside of this shop way too many times. The poor thing needed to be put to rest, but the owner was adamant on keeping it running, so who was I to argue? I would do everything in my power to keep this vehicle on the road. But thoughts of my ma were in the forefront of my mind, which made concentrating on these damn parts ten times harder.

Thirty more minutes had passed before the phone inside of the office started ringing. I looked up from my position underneath the dashboard of the old Chevy, willing the news on the other end of the line to be a good message coming from my father. I was slow to react, but I finally left my place from within the car to go answer the ringing contraption.

I tried to wipe the grease off of my hands as best I could with an old shop rag, and had to steady my shaking hand before I picked up the receiver. I just had the distinct feeling that whatever was on the other end wasn't going to be along the lines of good news.

What I wasn't expecting was it to be Hannah's school, informing me of a terrible accident involving my entire heart, my entire life. As the receiver slipped from my grasp and onto the floor, I'll be damned if I didn't feel as if it were my fault.

I changed my entire life, because of that one phone call that could've been prevented if I had chosen to do things differently.

CHAPTER 1

Sheridan

Present Day

Straining to open my eyes, the torturous pounding of my temples prevented my eyes from focusing. Trying to blink away the remnants of sleep, all I could see was white. Plain white walls and a white ceiling.

Where was I?

I tried to lift my head up off of the flat uncomfortable pillow in which it was resting on. Once I was able to raise it a fraction of an inch, my muscles screamed out in agony, that was when I noticed who was sitting in the chair towards the foot of my bed. A menacing scowl on his face as he stared daggers my way while his hands rested in his lap. I could just see the anger and hatred he felt towards me, dripping from his pores. He unclasped his hands and braced the arms of the chair as he pushed himself up to a standing position.

I warily watched his controlled movements, as he shuffled towards the head of my bed. My fingers dug into my blankets, bracing myself for the unknown. I never knew when or what would occur.

The closer he came, the faster my heart would beat.

Thump, thump, thump.

I had absolutely nowhere to go, I could only pray that he took it easy on me this time.

He slowly crept his face down to where his eyes were level with mine, I could see the fire burning in them down to the very depths of his soul. His gaze was so menacing, that if looks could actually kill, I would already be ten feet under.

Opening his mouth to no doubt give me one of his signature tongue lashings, I smelled the distinct smell of tequila, his liquor of choice. He was never nice to me anyways, but one would think as much as he drank it would affect his abilities and motor skills. I guess he had built up a tolerance to the stuff because if anything it made him meaner. And no one could ever tell him no. But it didn't used to be like this, alcohol was what made him into the monster he was today. One taste and he was hooked and there went my freedom, my happiness, and my life.

"Did you think you could actually run from me, Sheridan? Did you think that I wouldn't find you?" He moved even closer to where I had to close my eyes because he was invading my personal space, and putting me on the verge of a panic attack, which would only make things worse. He barked out, "Do you honestly think I'm that fucking stupid, Sheridan?"

"Nooo...no, sir," I stuttered. I always stuttered whenever he got like this. My entire thought logic went out the window and I was unable to form full, complete sentences, when normally I was a fairly intelligent individual who could hold my own in a conversation. That was my old life though, that was back in high school when I was carefree, a member of the band and the Captain of the Debate Team. Now, whenever he was around, he made me so scared and nervous that I would forget how to move and how to even breathe, and I didn't mean that in a good way.

I felt myself begin to thrash around in hopes he would just leave me alone for one day, my body ached and I didn't need the extra added abuse. Perhaps he would take pity on me. "Leave me alone, please." I heard myself scream.

Feeling two sets of hands wrap around my shoulders, my body registered the unwelcome feeling and began its process of shutting down. It was what I did during a beating or whatever he planned to do to me on that particular day. I would move into my inner comfort zone where nothing and no one could harm me, it was my inner protection, and completely tune out everything around me, it was safer that way. I didn't have to hear his onslaught of criticism regarding my body that he deemed 'his.' I was his slave, he was my master and how I should treat him as such. If he told me to open my legs, that I better do it, or I was in for a world of hurt, even more so than would occur if I just obeyed his every command. I didn't know what passionate sex or love making was anymore. Once upon a time there was a time and place when I enjoyed it, but now it was just a command that I needed to obey in order to live to see another day. I didn't know whether he was capable of murder, but he had come close several times in the years before.

"Sheridan," I heard a deep voice say, but this wasn't *his* voice. This voice was gentle and laced with concern and made me want to open my eyes. I fought my hardest to come out of personal protection mode so I could see who was so concerned with my well-being. "Sheridan, wake up. You're having a bad dream." I heard that serene voice say again.

I tried to catch my breath as I opened my eyes to see the most beautiful pair of hazel eyes staring back at me. I felt as if I could've just openly stared into them for the remainder of the day. I, unfortunately, had to blink which lost the intense connection between the other set of eyes. I looked around only to end up having everything from the previous day come back to me.

Me leaving my home outside Atlanta to try and start a new life for myself. Getting into an accident by a drunk driver in a small Podunk town, which led me to why I was currently lying in a bed in the hospital with a broken foot and my ribs screaming at me from the pain. And the man who was calling my name was still standing by my bedside; the man who I didn't know why he was being so nice to me; the man with sadness written all over his entire face; the man with the beautiful eyes, Mike Jameson.

"Sheridan are you alright?" he asked, his eyes roaming the entire length of my body.

"Uh yes," I stated, using the remote to raise the hospital bed to where I could sit up a little better, "I'm fine, thank you. Must have been a bad dream, no big deal." I was hoping he would take my nonchalance about the dream and move on.

Mike was the paramedic who got me out of my car after an asshole drunk proceeded to use it as a battering ram, while I was waiting at a stop light. I had absolutely no idea why he kept coming to check on me, it wasn't as if I were his responsibility.

Every other time he'd come in, he was in his uniform and it was bad enough that he looked gorgeous in it, but the man in just plain street attire had my breath whooshing out of my lungs. He was dressed in a pair of faded jeans with a long sleeved, unbuttoned flannel shirt with a navy t-shirt underneath. His shirt sleeves were rolled up to expose his muscular forearms, arms that looked strong and would protect. On top of his head, he had an old tattered navy baseball cap. It had certainly seen better days, I guess he was a man who couldn't part with his favorite hat.

I hadn't had a man be nice to me in a long time, it was a comforting thought, but one I couldn't allow myself to dwell on or think it made any sort of difference. I was tainted goods, I needed to remember that. I had a mission, and looking down towards my booted foot, it would be a hindrance, but I still needed to remember what I was doing. Getting away from an old, bad life and trying to make a new one. Only now, I was stuck in Brown County, Georgia with no car and no place to go.

I needed to get to the bottom of why Mike was being so nice to me, he didn't know me and apparently now with the way he was dressed, he had come visit me while on his day off.

I glanced up at him to see him staring at my lips. I absentmindedly darted my tongue out to wet the object of his fixation. His pupils flared as he inhaled a deep breath. "Mike," I said which had him snapping out of his trance and looking me in the eyes, "why are you being so nice to me?" I had to put it bluntly, I didn't like to beat around the bush, I had to tiptoe around my words too much before and I'll be damned if I had to do it in my new life as well.

He slid his hands into his pockets and slightly lifted a shoulder. Not much of an answer, but I guess that was all I was going to get.

I opened my mouth to ask yet another question, when I was interrupted by the doctor. "Miss Nichols?" he asked, and it almost didn't register until it was too late that he was addressing me.

Right, I'm Miss Nichols…

Giving my undivided attention to Dr. Wallace, who was pretty handsome as well, *what did they feed these men in Brown County?* Everywhere I turned, there was a sweet, attractive man. I couldn't help but think, I should've came barreling into Brown County years ago, then I could have dodged all of the abuse and heartache I've had to deal with.

Seeing the good doctor just stand there, I realized that he was waiting for my response. "Oh, yes, I'm sorry. Go on."

"Well," he said snapping open my file and shutting it again, "your CT scan came back clear, so there is no need for you to stay in the hospital another night, that is if that's what you want?"

I didn't hesitate in voicing my displeasure about being cooped up inside a hospital. "Yes, sir, I'd like to get out of here." I had already been worried about how much this hospital stay would cost until I learned that it would be covered by the asshole who hit me. Now, I would have to hail a cab and find a decent hotel to sleep in for a few days, until I could figure out what I was going to do next.

"Very good, Miss Nichols. Now even though your scan was clear, you did suffer some severely bruised ribs, a broken foot, and several scrapes and abrasions, you'll need someone to stay with you, or else I can't permit you to leave."

What the hell?

I didn't have anyone, not anyone here anyways. I immediately closed my gaping mouth that had fallen open after he dropped that bomb on me. "Why? I don't have…"

"I'll be sure to look after her." Mike said making me snap my head in his direction, which in turn caused my head to scream out in pain.

"No, I can't…I can't ask you to do that, Mike."

He walked forward just a step or two, *I shrank back into my bed. Why on earth was he trying to get close to me?* He placed his hands on the rails of my hospital bed and leaned down to where he was a hairsbreadth away. Normally I would be frightened, for a man to be so close to me, but the concern and empathy that shone in his eyes made me feel, oddly reassured. "You didn't ask me to, Sheridan." He quickly stood back up, and moved away from me almost as if he were to spend too much time in my personal space it would harm him. He moved towards Dr. Wallace, "Sheridan will be coming home with me."

While the two men in the room shook hands, I wondered if I actually had a say in any of this. Shouldn't it ultimately be my decision whether or not I wanted to be brought home by this perpetual stranger? It was April first I believe, was this some kind of sick joke? Yeah, well I'm not laughing.

And even though my red flags weren't alerting me of potential danger, that didn't mean I should automatically trust him either.

I thought back to my other visitor from this morning, Maggie, and I wondered if I could call her to come pick me up instead.

Maggie Walker was a trauma nurse here at the hospital, she and her boyfriend were witnesses to the wreck. She didn't hesitate in coming to my aid after seeing the humungous truck careening towards me.

She snapped into action, making her way into the backseat of my damaged car and securing my head in place until Mike and the ambulance arrived.

She was also able to talk me off of the ledge of a major panic attack and keep me calm until help arrived.

Maggie made an intense situation a little bit more manageable given the circumstances.

She came by to make sure I was alright which was so sweet of her. It also gave me the opportunity to thank her for going above and beyond the call of duty. At first when she arrived, I was on the phone and I didn't notice her come in. I was hoping she didn't catch much of my phone conversation between my mother and me.

Only staying for a few minutes, she ended up leaving but not before giving me her number. I could very well call her and see if she would bring me to a nearby hotel and no one would be the wiser.

Shit, she was a nurse and more than likely followed doctor's orders. I couldn't put her in that situation.

I guess I was stuck going home with Mike. What's the worst that could happen, it wasn't like I would fall for the guy…

CHAPTER 2

Mike

What the fuck was wrong with me?

I didn't only make a continuous effort to visit the starry-eyed goddess, but now I was offering up my house and volunteering to take care of her?

The only logical reasoning that I could even remotely come up with would be that I had an incredible case of lust. That or some kind of shape shifter was taking over my body.

I'd admit that I felt an instant connection to Sheridan, but I couldn't let anything occur from that attraction. I've lost too much in my life for another woman to swoop in and dig her claws into me.

I'd be better off dropping her off at a nearby hotel, but I wasn't that big of an asshole.

Controlling my urge to take her would be especially tough when she was so near, but I would have to fight it tooth and nail.

Once I shook hands with Dr. Wallace, I looked over at Sheridan who had her mouth hanging wide open.

I furrowed my brows and asked tersely, "What?" It came out a bit more harshly than I intended.

A stunned look appeared on her face and she quickly shook it away. "Nothing. Uh…thank you." She added softly.

I needed to get away from her to regroup and get my shit together. "Do you have a suitcase or other belongings?" She had briefly told me that she was on her way someplace, but didn't specify where. I assumed she would've brought extra clothes with her, if so I was going to retrieve them from where her car is now.

"Yah, I had a duffel bag with me, but I guess it's still in my car." She brought her hands to the top of her head, "Oh no, where is my car?"

"Your car is in the local salvage yard. It's considered totaled, which means it can't be fixed."

"Well, how do you know this?" I imagined that if she were standing, she'd have her hands on her hips.

"I'm a mechanic. I've been working on cars for almost half of my life. And there is absolutely no fixing that car, the axel is broken from the impact and the entire driver's side is beyond repair. It would cost more to be fixed than what the car is actually worth."

Her face fell as if she had been scolded, I guess I did respond rather sternly. "Oh, ok." She looked down at the light blue blanket that was covering her lower extremities and began fiddling with a frayed edge.

In this position, she looked too small and vulnerable. I needed to remember to keep myself in check and watch my tone with her. After all, it wasn't her fault that she was the first woman I'd been really attracted to since Erin. I just couldn't act on that attraction.

"While you are getting discharged, I'll go get your belongings out of your car, I brought you some sweats and one of my T-shirts. They may swallow you but, it'll be better than showing all of the elderly patients your exposed backside and giving them heart palpitations."

She peeked up at me, a quizzical expression on her face. It was supposed to make her smile and instead it just backfired on me. I should just stick to being broody. "Never mind," I shook it off. "I'll be back in a bit."

Forty-five minutes later, I was pulling up to the main entrance of the hospital, now with an oversized duffel, musical keyboard, an old photo album, and a cell phone car charger. That was the extent of her belongings that was in the car.

I opened my door and hopped out of my truck the same time a nurse rolled Sheridan out in a wheelchair.

Opening the passenger door, she tried to stand, putting most of her weight on her right leg. She had to quickly tug up the sweats I lent her, as they were too big, even with her rolling the waist down several times, and tried hobbling towards the opened door. They ended up letting her have a walking boot since she had injured ribs, the crutches would only further aggravate them.

The cast on her left foot went up to the middle of her calf and was big and bulky.

Taking her first real look at my truck, she turned her attention towards me, her eyebrows almost disappearing into her hairline.

"How do you expect me to get up in this thing?" she asked as she flicked her wrist at my truck and lifted her lip in distaste.

I was completely shocked, *did she just insult my truck?* Women *loved* my truck. It was a damn good thing I wasn't going to act on my attraction, because that just pissed me the fuck off.

"Yeah, it's not a *thing*," I scoffed. "It's a 2010 Ford F-150 FX4, which means it is several thousand pounds of badass. I modded it myself, putting on a six inch lift kit and replaced the original grill for a chrome one; it also has a Flowmaster exhaust among numerous other modifications." I schooled her as if she knew what exactly I was saying.

Sheridan held her hands up in surrender, looking a bit lost, "Um...ok. Let me rephrase that, how am I supposed to get up in this big ass, black truck?" She then raised her eyebrows as if daring me to give a rebuttal.

I let out an exasperated sigh. It wouldn't do me a damn bit of good to get frustrated. Taking off my baseball cap and running my fingers through my short cropped hair, I further thought about how this wasn't the best idea. Replacing my hat, I went up behind Sheridan and grasped her around her waist. Hearing her sharp intake of breath, I wanted nothing more than to continue to hold her in my embrace.

Alas, I thought better of it and hoisted her up into my truck, being cautious of her foot.

Rounding the back of my truck, I had to stop at the tailgate to take a deep, cleansing breath. It would be my last one for a while since her scent would be filling my truck and house.

How would I be able to resist her while she was in my personal space?

Not wanting to be gone too long for her to get suspicious, I easily lifted myself into the driver's side seat and fired up The Beast.

I spent all of my extra time now working on my truck, which between becoming a paramedic, working at Ray's Garage on the side, and being drummer for The Nation's Capital, it didn't end up being much. But it beat sitting in an empty house, well empty except for Sadie. I found that if I sat for too long my mind would wander to things that I had no control over. So, I made sure to keep busy.

When I moved to Brown County three and a half years ago, the first thing I did was buy a house and worked round the clock fixing it to my liking. Living in a house that I remodeled with my own two hands gave me a sense of satisfaction, knowing that I did it without having any input from a woman was refreshing.

Glancing out of the corner of my eye, I saw Sheridan slumped in her seat with her elbow perched on the door frame, looking out the window.

It bothered me that I actually wanted to know what she was thinking about. What was going on in her head at this exact moment? Was she thinking about me? What was she running away from? She couldn't fool me, I knew she was running from something or someone.

Giving my undivided attention back to the road, I had to uncurl my hands from the death grip they had on my steering wheel. I was anxious and nervous, and those weren't two emotions I liked feeling. Pissed, complacent, moody, those were feelings I could handle, all the others that actually made you *feel* were unchartered territory for me now.

I decided that I shouldn't be an asshole and at least try to engage in some kind of conversation. There was one thing that occurred earlier that had been constantly on my mind.

"Who or what is Pate?"

Sheridan whipped her head around so fast she could've actually gotten whiplash from the sheer force of her movement. I chanced a glance in her direction to see the horrified expression on her face. "Why did you ask that?" There was even a tremor in her voice.

"You were whimpering in your sleep saying 'No, Pate,' so I was just wondering who or what Pate was." I answered while shrugging one of my shoulders.

"Oh... Nothing, it's nothing. Don't worry about it." She turned back to where she was looking out the window, but this time she was chewing on a fingernail.

Alright then, I guess simple conversation was off of the table. Just as well though, I might end up saying something I'd regret.

An overwhelming vanilla aroma assaulted me. Her scent

had already seeped into the cab of my truck, home could not come any faster.

Taking a liberal whiff, I wanted to commit her fragrance to memory, I wanted more.

Shaking my head, trying to get rid of the nonsense that kept popping up in my thoughts. *It's because you are so close to her, just keep your distance but not enough to be considered inhospitable and things should be alright.*

I had to get her intoxicating smell out of the confines of my truck. I pressed the buttons on my door panel to roll the windows down. It was a nice enough day out that hopefully she wouldn't complain. That was definitely one thing I enjoy living without, a woman complaining.

Erin would bitch and nitpick about every little fucking thing. Just thinking about her made my blood begin to boil. This was why I kept busy, why I always had some kind of noise in the background to distract me from my thoughts running amuck.

Reaching over I pushed the radio dial to turn on some music to fill the silence in the truck and to drown out the chaos that ensued in my head. "Maneater" by Hall & Oates was playing on the airwaves and wasn't that a downright coincidence. I bet Sheridan was a maneater, trying to come off all innocent. I looked over at Sheridan who had her arm stuck out the window, making a wave motion with her hand cutting through the wind.

Her long, unsecured black hair, so dark that it reminded me of midnight, was whipping around in the breeze. It made me wish for things I had absolutely no right wishing for. I wanted to run my fingers through her wild hair, combing through the dishevelment, to feel her silky strands go through my rough, overworked hands. I felt a tiny pang in my chest because I could never let myself have that closeness ever again, it just wasn't a possibility and above all else, I didn't deserve it.

I was thankful for the center console that was between us.

It was a good reminder that I needed to put a halt on my desires. I deserved to live my life alone with my guilt.

But having Sheridan stay with me, sure wouldn't make this easy.

CHAPTER 3

Sheridan

After what felt like forever, he turned down a street that ended in a cul-de-sac aligned with different types of houses. It appealed to me that it wasn't a cookie cutter neighborhood, each house looking the exact same. Finally, he drove around the circle drive and pulled into the last house on the left. It was a one-story gray brick ranch style home with a navy blue front door and shutters.

He sure had a thing for the color.

The lawn was mowed close in a vertically angled pattern and the landscaping looked professionally done. But if the grease and dirt stains around his cuticles and nail beds were any indication, he liked to get his hands dirty. I had no doubt in my mind that he did this job himself, and what he had created, was art.

Different types of shrubbery lined the outside of the house and beautiful, vibrant spring flowers flowed alongside his driveway and wrapped around his mailbox.

Somehow seeing such a beautiful, put together home

made me breathe just a bit easier. I had no idea why I trusted Mike as much as I did, he was often rude and always seemed angry.

I was walking blindly into this whole situation. Who knew what awaited on the other side of his navy blue door, but I guaranteed it would be better than what I'd come from.

"Are you just going to sit there all day?"

Looking at the empty driver's seat, I turned to see Mike holding open my door. I was so lost in thought that I completely missed him getting out, let alone opening my door.

I turned to where my body was facing his, I knew he was going to have to help me out, which meant his hands would be on me again.

Quickly, I tried to brace myself, but no amount of preparation could equip me in feeling his immediate heat. The electricity from his fingertips zapped straight to my core, making me want things, that given my history, I'd be crazy to want.

His hands lingered on my hips a little longer than most deemed appropriate, but I wasn't going to complain, it wasn't in my nature. At long last, I looked up through my lashes, recognizing the heat in his eyes. His intense hazel irises dilated and turned just a fraction more green which made them look even more beautiful than before.

He seemed to be holding his breath and dropped his hands hastily. Luckily, I was able to grab on to the door handle since I hadn't been able to properly regain my balance.

Going about his business, he grabbed my duffle and started walking towards the house.

I honestly didn't know how long I would be able to stay here. Hopefully, within a day or two, he would have felt like he fulfilled his volunteer duty and let me find a hotel to stay in.

I took slow, controlled steps until I made it to the base of his front porch.

I studied the concrete slabs that led to his house and had no idea how I was going to get up them. Mike had already went inside so he was of no use. I really wondered what had crawled up his ass. If he didn't want me here, then why even volunteer? It wasn't as if the doctor twisted his arm. Sheesh.

Looking at the steps once again, I contemplated yelling for Mike to get his ass back out here and help me, but I was a new self-sufficient woman. I could do this on my own.

Using the railing on his porch as a brace, I tried getting up each step, putting as minimal weight on my casted foot as possible and said numerous obscenities during each one. The movement heading up the stairs made my pain so severe in my ribs that they were actually burning, this entire trip wasn't an easy one to take. At least when Mike was getting me in and out of his truck, the heat from his skin made me overlook the pain. You'd think someone as familiar to pain as I was, that I would be able to bear it a little bit better, but no such luck.

Once I cleared all three steps, I felt the need to do a little dance, but Mr. Moody probably forbade something like that taking place on his property.

Finally having made it into the house, I saw my belongings dumped on the floor, but no Mike, so I went on my search of finding him.

His living room was to the right of the entryway and was decorated with neutral colors. A black leather couch was in the middle of the floor situated in front of a big screen TV that was mounted to the wall. He had a few decorative pieces hung on the walls, such as a mirror and a giant clock, but nothing that showed who he was as a person. Not a single picture frame or family photo.

My foot was feeling quite sore and I felt fatigued, so I quickly trudged through on my search in trying to find Mike.

It almost felt as if I were snooping in Mike's house, but someone wasn't very hospitable, so I wasn't really left with a choice.

His dining room was down the hall from the entryway and connected to his kitchen.

I could see stainless steel appliances in his kitchen, but that wasn't what initially caught my attention. It was the enormous bay window that overlooked a tropical oasis. The bench was calling my name, all of the welcoming pillows drew me directly to it.

I unconsciously went and sat down on the bench and peered through the open curtain into his gorgeous backyard.

An oasis was the perfect word to describe what I was seeing. If I thought that the front yard was a work of art, then the backyard was a masterpiece.

A pleasant, peaceful, and tranquil place to unwind after the stress of the day.

The wooden pergola was what first caught my attention. The sun shining down through the wooden beams and onto his patio, which housed a furniture set, grill, and a fire pit.

My eyes continued on the journey, trying to take in every little bit of detail.

There were numerous bushes, shrubs, and flowers that were crowded in rows along his property line, and you could just faintly see his privacy fence through some of the branches of the trees.

His grass was so vibrant, the greenest I had ever seen.

I felt as if I could just take up residence right here, in his backyard. I would definitely never run out of beautiful things to look at. All it needed was a... Well, what do you know, he had a hammock as well.

In the very back corner of his property, nestled in between two overgrown oak trees, was a large rope hammock. I could just imagine lying in it and watching the clouds as the day passed by.

But currently, it was being occupied by Mike, who was

sitting up and bent over at the waist, rubbing a dog's head. A beautiful chocolate lab, which instantly brought a smile to my face.

Just the way they interacted together, it brought new meaning to the phrase, *man's best friend.*

I felt myself drawing nearer to the window, wanting to be closer to their happy moment. I wanted to see what it would be like to be *happy* even if just for a few measly minutes.

I placed both of my hands on the window pane so I could continue peering at their welcome home reunion. I had stooped to an all-time low, actually wanting to be part of the happiness and camaraderie between pet and owner. I was officially pathetic.

Being engrossed in my deplorable pity party, I didn't realize that Mike's eyes were currently boring holes into mine.

He caught me literally red-handed gawking at him. I removed my hands from their position on the window and rubbed them on my oversized borrowed clothes.

It warmed my heart that he actually thought to bring me something to wear. Between that and him springing that joke on me, it had caught me completely off guard.

He stood from the hammock and began walking towards the backdoor, the mutt hot on his heels. I hoped to God that he wouldn't mention my little onlooker session.

I turned to where my back was now to the window and I was able to get a good look at the kitchen since the backyard demanded my attention first.

One thing I noticed as I studied his setup was that he was unusually clean. I sincerely hoped that I wasn't intruding on him and his girlfriend. I didn't want to be a burden and interfere. I didn't see a ring or an outline on his left hand, not that I looked too terribly hard. Ok, that was a lie. I looked every chance I got to see if there was a tan line marking of a ring.

The next thing I knew I was being accosted by a very cold

nose and an incredibly wet tongue.

Seeing the dog's tail wag unrelentingly back and forth, I knew the dog was happy I was here.

"Sadie, get down," Mike scolded.

I started rubbing her all over her dark brown coat and then scratching behind her ears. "It's alright Sadie Belle," I cooed in a more soprano tone. "You are just excited to see someone different, maybe even a little more friendly. Oh, it's been so long since I've been allowed to have a dog. Who's a pretty girl?" I continued scratching her head, as she pushed her head against my hand.

"Why weren't you allowed to have a dog?" Mike asked while leaning against his countertop with his arms folded across his chest.

"Oh, because he..." Then I stopped myself before I disclosed any more information. I wasn't about to delve deep into my past, I already almost blew it when I talked about Pate during my nightmare. For some strange reason, I didn't want to see pity and hatred on Mike's face being directed towards me. So I quickly recovered, "My ex was allergic." I averted my eyes from his scrutiny and turned my attention back towards Sadie.

"Right," he said as if he saw right through my lie, "and her name is Sadie, not Sadie Belle!" he chastised me as if I were a child instead of a fully grown woman. He was definitely not a ray of sunshine by any means and I was frankly tired of his rudeness.

I stood from my position on the bench and moved a few steps in his direction where he stood in the kitchen.

My heart was slamming against my ribs because I had never been one to stand up in a confrontation, but the journey was supposed to be me turning over a new leaf, starting over, and not being anyone's doormat any longer. It was my time to be *brave*.

I raised my index finger and thrust it towards his face and

tried my hardest to sound stern, "Why do you have to be so rude?" I yelled in his face. "I didn't ask to come here! I have been told what to do basically for the last eight years of my life. Now, we can both forget about all of this and you can just take me to the nearest hotel. Or, if you are too busy to take me, please just point me in the direction of my room and I will call a cab in the morning. My pain medicine is wearing off and my foot is throbbing so I wouldn't be in your way." I let out an exasperated sigh, I was just tired of being treated like shit from someone who knew me all of five minutes.

"Oh my God!" talk about a delayed reaction, you would think my spidey senses would be on hyper alert after my past situations, but I felt so safe with Mike. *How could I be so stupid?*

I'm sure I had a horrified expression on my face, because Mike pushed himself off the counter and began advancing on me.

"What's wrong, Sheridan? Is it your foot?" He genuinely sounded concerned, which was a pleasant change from him being a pompous asshole.

"Well, my foot is aching, but I've dealt with much worse. I just realized why you are being such a fucking douche to me!"

His brows pierced together as if he were challenging me to confront him.

"You are going to murder me in my sleep!" His jaw dropped open and he looked like he had a million and one things to say, but it seemed as if I had stunned him speechless. I continued on, placing a hand on my hip. "No, seriously, that's why you were so adamant about me coming with you."

Finally, he seemed to come unglued as he threw his head back and let out a barreling laugh that came from deep within his gut.

Seeing him release such a hearty belly laugh at my concern should have royally pissed me off, but instead it did the complete opposite, it turned me on. A rush of wetness flooded from my core, instantly soaking my panties.

It had been so long since a man had invoked such a positive and sexual reaction from me.

I had to tamp down my lust and remember that he was a cocky jerk and things would be just dandy.

"You actually think that I brought you here to kill you in your sleep? Chop you up into tiny little pieces and shove you down my garbage disposal? You are delusional, maybe your concussion is affecting you more than you initially thought."

My hand was still placed on my hip while my other was balled tightly into a fist and I tapped my good foot mercilessly on the floor. He technically hadn't answered me and I wasn't going to stand down until I was thoroughly convinced. His explanation seemed a little too well thought out if it was just a spur of the moment.

"That's not the reason I brought you here, Sheridan. And besides, my house doesn't even have a garbage disposal, which, therefore, makes my plan void." He shrugged as if I was the absurd one.

I relaxed just a fraction, but that didn't answer my question of why. "Then why did you volunteer to bring me here?" I crossed my arms in front of my chest, which showcased a white bandage taped on my forearm, covering the biggest abrasion from the flying shards of glass.

He came a beat closer, quickly closing in the bit of distance between us. I instinctively took a step back, trying to widen that gap. I couldn't risk him getting closer to me, if I were to get a better whiff of his spicy scent, I would sure be a goner, and I needed to stand my ground.

"Sweetheart, I haven't a clue, but when you've hatched another ridiculous theory, be sure to fill me in." He said in a low, cocky and condescending tone.

I really thought he liked provoking me. He wanted to see

22

fire, well he was about to get a taste of his own rudeness and go up in flames.

"The name is Sheridan, not sweetheart. I'm not now, nor will I ever be *your* sweetheart. Now, please do me a solid and point me in the direction of my room for the night. I'll be out of your way first thing in the morning." I may have looked strong on the outside, but on the inside I was shaking like a flimsy leaf getting ready to be blown into the wind. I would never be able to hold my own in a fight, it was too scary and intimidating. No wonder why I always submitted to Pate... *Stop thinking about him.*

He said not a word as he shuffled past me and led me back through the hallway towards the entryway to retrieve my duffle. He went through the living room and down another hallway that had two doors on the right and one on the left. Opening one of the doors on the right, he brought my duffle and sat it down on the bed and walked around me and was out of sight.

This was an extremely bad idea to come here, in leaving my parents' house altogether, but if I was going to make a new life, I needed a new place to call home. It was just my luck that I would be blindsided in a wreck and stuck here for God knows how long.

After I went to a hotel in the morning, I needed to find a replacement mode of transportation. My mom wasn't happy to hear that I had broken yet another bone, stuck in a strange town, and wanted me home immediately. I couldn't though, go home, it wasn't safe.

I closed the door then sat my keyboard on top of the white painted dresser. Taking a look around the room it was just like the rest of the house, clean. I very much liked that he didn't feel the need to be the normal statistic for a man, having a cluttered house with dishes piled high in the kitchen and empty beer bottles littering the coffee table. The guest bedroom was done in all white furniture. I was surprised to see that the comforter didn't reflect his love of the color navy blue as it was crisply made with a red and white checkered gingham print bedspread. I couldn't wait another minute, I flung myself down on the bed and sunk my toes of my unbooted foot into the fibers of the carpet below me.

Enjoying the luxury of a soft mattress for the night would be the highlight of my week. Then I would have to settle into some hard ass hotel bed for a few days until everything got situated. At least the accommodations at the hotel would be better than what I was used to. I just needed to keep thinking positive thoughts; things were headed in the right direction. Everyone hit a few bumps on the way to their happy ever after, even though I've encountered some rather large pot holes, the kind that would pop your tire, good things were bound to come.

I hoped.

CHAPTER 4

Mike

Sitting in one of my wooden dining room chairs, my elbows on the table, and my head cradled in my hands, I reflected over the last few minutes. Leave it to me to be a world class asshole to Sheridan, it wasn't her fault that I was attracted to her. I felt like a high school bully, picking on the girl who I had a crush on because I was too much of a pansy to let her in on my attraction.

She kept dropping not so subtle hints on things I really didn't know how to grasp. Talking about not being *allowed* to do something and having to follow commands for the last eight years. The worst comment she made was that she has had much worse than a broken foot, I didn't know how to articulate that. Someone or something had harmed Sheridan and it made my blood boil just to think that.

That girl had some serious skeletons in her closet and I was just adding to that fuel by being a dick. I needed to come up with a new plan on what to do, I wasn't going to let her just take off in some unknown town, and I couldn't keep being an asshole to her. And I very well couldn't be around her and act on my lust craze that I had on her either. I think the best thing to do was just keep my distance. Perhaps they will have some extra shifts for me to pick up at work, or maybe an overabundance of cars will come into Ray's that need to be fixed.

I heard a piano playing very faintly coming from the back of my house so I raised my head and straightened my slumped body. It was a sad song, extremely melancholy. I found myself instinctively rising from my chair and walking towards my guest bedroom so I could listen a little better. The song that Sheridan was playing, I remembered hearing in one of my several music classes that I took growing up, Beethoven's "Moonlight Sonata."

My heart hurt just listening to the tune filled with so much despair.

This was absolutely no song for a beginner, so she must know her way around the keys of a piano. Although, her keyboard was a top of the line model, it was still no match for a true actual well-tuned piano.

I raised my hand to knock on the door, wanting to apologize for my rudeness, but I stopped short and just rested my outstretched hand against the smooth grain of the wood.

I couldn't tell you why I hesitated, because I didn't understand it myself. A knot had formed in the pit of my stomach at the thought of her upset because of my actions, but it wouldn't do a bit of good for me to go make nice with her. She would just see that as an open invitation to get close to me which was no longer an option. I don't let people in, but damn if I didn't kind of like the idea of letting her inside.

I couldn't listen to this music, it was making me feel even more vulnerable. It wasn't helping in drowning out the emptiness that was inside of me. I needed to get out of here and away from the feelings of longing and wanting something more.

Hopefully, Emmy Lou's wouldn't have much of a crowd.

26

I didn't want to deal with crazy women, flaunting their shit, wanting a chance.

Or perhaps, that was exactly what I needed.

A willing and able warm body, available for a no-strings attached quick fuck. They would know the score and hopefully that would satiate my desire to take Sheridan.

Yeah, I think that would do it, it had been awhile since I'd plunged my dick into a tight, hot pussy.

Thinking I held the magical solution to all of my problems, I had an extra pep in my step as I went to take a quick shower and get ready to go out on my quest to get laid.

I made quick time in washing and rinsing my body. With the exhaust fan on in the bathroom, I couldn't hear the keyboard. So imagine my surprise when I dart out of the bathroom, with nothing but a towel wrapped around my waist and ran straight into Sheridan, making said towel slip out of my grasp as I grabbed her forearms to steady her balance.

"I'm sorry Sheridan, I wasn't looking where I was going." I apologized, still holding onto her soft flesh. She had changed out of my clothes that swallowed her and into a red tank and plaid pajama pants.

She started backing up, making me drop my arms down to my sides. Having yet to look at me, I glanced down towards the floor to try and see what her eyes were trained on. Not even realizing that I was now in the nude showing off my now twitching cock at the thought of it being under Sheridan's stare.

I bent down to grab my abandoned towel and quickly replaced it around my waist before her gaze snapped up to mine.

The heat in her eyes was overwhelmingly evident. She wasn't unaffected by the sight of me, her lack of a response told me that.

"I wouldn't want this if I were you." I tried to sound snotty. Maybe if I could ward her off of me it would make things easier on me.

She arched her brow and curled up a corner of her mouth in disgust before she hastily bit out, "Oh, please stop flattering yourself." And she whirled around into the bathroom and slammed the door.

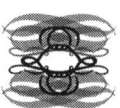

Emmy Lou's had a pretty decent crowd tonight, lots of women to choose from. I settled myself on an available bar stool and raised my hand signaling that I needed a beer.

Moments later, Charlie Hennings appeared with an ice cold bottle of Heineken that he had just popped the top on before sitting it on a napkin in front of me. With a brief jerk of my head portraying my appreciation, he went on about his work.

Charlie was newer around here, being settled here just a little over a year. He was a replacement bass player in our band, The Nation's Capital, and was currently dating Maggie Walker who was the trauma nurse who was on the scene to help Sheridan just moments after her wreck occurred.

He was a good guy as far as I could tell, he knew I wasn't much for idle chitchat, so he normally let me be.

The one person who I could tolerate around here was Brock Monroe, the other guitarist in the band and the closest thing to a friend I had. He didn't pry into my past and I didn't have to make excuses to him. He was there if and when I needed him.

Now his wife Tessa, on the other hand, never passed up an opportunity to bust my balls and the look she was currently giving me from the other end of the bar tonight was no different. And why would it be?

Tessa also worked at Emmy Lou's, although she had considerably cut back on her hours after she had her and

Brock's son, Blake.

"Well, well, lookie what the cat drug in…"

"Now, Tessa, you couldn't have missed me too much, you saw me Saturday night." I said as I took a pull from my beer.

"Oh, you mean when you'd dashed in right before the show started? Or when I saw the back of your head as you were quicker than a flash of lightning getting out of here after the last song? What gives?"

Tessa was never one to let things go and I wasn't one to divulge, so we were at a stalemate.

I said nothing as I stood from the stool, retrieved my beer and found an empty table as far from the bar and Tessa as I could find.

I was doing good keeping Sheridan off of my mind and Tessa had to bring up Saturday.

The show she was referring to took place this past Saturday. It was one of our first shows in months. Tessa had just had Blake so Brock had to start putting in extra hours at Ray's Auto Shop to help compensate Tess's lack of hours since she'd had a newborn at home. We all decided it'd be best if we took a break from playing. We were a hot band around here and it took some more convincing for others, but ultimately we were at a draw.

Since it had been awhile since we had performed last, the bar was jam packed to the brim and we ended up playing a kickass show. The energy in Emmy Lou's was at an all-time high, but I just couldn't bring myself to get into it because coincidentally it was also the same day Sheridan was introduced to Brown County by way of a car accident. I couldn't stick around and have a below mediocre time when I could've been watching over Sheridan in the hospital.

She had spent most of the time in and out of sleep and groggy due to the pain medicine they were administering. Which was fine by me, it had given me a chance to study the soft, intricate lines of her face, I could almost guarantee that it would be smooth under my touch. The way her lashes fanned out across her cheeks. And the way her lips were parted just a fraction of an inch as she took steady, deep breaths.

Something about her drew me in. She had me, hook, line, and sinker. *No! How could you even remotely think that would be wise? Falling for another woman, only to have it end in heartache.* I was hopeless.

A hand caressing my shoulder pulled me out of my internal war.

I looked up into the eyes of Tracy, a nefarious busybody who everyone warned you to stay away from. She was often relentless in her pursuit to get into my pants, hell to get into the pants of any man, and with the heat that was flaring in her eyes, tonight was no exception.

Normally, I wouldn't touch her with a ten foot pole, but I seriously needed a release if I was going to try and keep my distance from Sheridan.

"Hey, Tracy," I mumbled as I took another generous swig of my beer, if I was going to actually have a conversation with her I needed to be a little less lucid.

"Hi, Mikey," she said, trying to sound seductive but having failed miserably. She was pretty in her own right, but her blonde locks did nothing for me when all that was on my mind was the black tresses of Sheridan.

And seriously what was with everyone calling me Mikey? My name was Mike. It irritated me to no end that people thought we were buddy enough for them to give me a nickname. Which was strictly not the case.

She leaned down closer to my ear to where her open shirt exposing her full, rounded cleavage was staring me right in the face. Taking the tip of one of her well-manicured nails she dragged her finger down my chest almost to my crotch. I actually squirmed wanting her to touch my very quickly inflating erection. Opening her mouth and releasing an extremely hot breath at my ear, she said, "Are you looking for some company tonight, honey?"

The honey statement was all it took for me to remember where I was and who I was with. I wasn't her or anyone else's 'honey.' Damn, why did she have to open her mouth and kill my mood before it even really got started?

But before I knew it, I was being dragged into the men's restroom, and I'll admit, I was going pretty willingly. A few men were gathered in the entrance and immediately snickered once they saw Tracy entering with me in tow. They weren't stupid, they knew what was going on.

She shoved me into the farthest stall and once she locked the door, she shoved me up against the cool, concrete tiled wall. Pushing up on her toes and trying to attack my mouth, I turned my face away. I wasn't going to kiss her, that wasn't what this was about. To me, a kiss was an intimate moment and I wouldn't let her think that this was going to be something that it undoubtedly wasn't.

After a few seconds, she got the hint and after a brief, agitated sigh she started fumbling with the buckle on my belt. Setting the belt free, she rushed at unbuttoning my jeans and lowering the teeth on my zipper. Normally I would have done all of this myself, but it was quite amusing seeing her get all riled up. I think she had finally gotten it into her head that I wasn't in here for a quick fuck, nope. As much of a dick as it made me, this wasn't about her, this was about my release. I wouldn't go anywhere near her pussy with my dick; no matter how much I needed a release. Knowing her and as much as she got around it would be like throwing a hotdog down a hallway, and I'd rather have a tight, hot pussy to sink into.

"Aren't you going to touch me, honey?" she whined as her hands rimmed the edges of my boxer briefs.

And there she went with the honey thing again. I felt my

anger spiking and I was about to get extremely blunt and not in a good way.

"Tracy, the way I'm feeling right now, I would be completely too rough." Not exactly a lie, but also nowhere near the entire truth either. "What I need from you is for you to quit talking and take my rock hard cock and wrap your mouth around it. Do you think you can do that for me, or should I go back out into the bar and find a willing participant?" I quirked a brow, daring her to tell me no.

She rolled her eyes and I was almost expecting her to defy me, but at the last minute before I began fastening my jeans, she gripped the edges of the fabric and yanked them down to my ankles, letting my dick spring free.

Pausing before she began her assault on my dick, I watched as her eyes flared and her pink lips parted as she took in a sharp inhalation of breath. Her tongue darted out and licked her lips, wetting them and my dick jumped in appreciation. She was impressed with my size and I was anxiously awaiting my dick being in the hot, wet recess of her mouth momentarily. At least she had better hurry up, before I started taking matters into my own hands.

"Are you going to suck my dick, or are you just going to sit there and stare at it all night?" I really didn't know where this asshole side of me was coming from. I had never spoken to a woman like this, and I almost regretted it. Almost.

She looked up into my eyes, her dark blue orbs smiling as she grabbed ahold of my erection and licked it from the base to the tip before taking it deep within her mouth.

I closed my eyes and slammed my head back against the wall, and released a guttural grunt, whether it was from the pain from the blow or the feeling of my dick getting attention, I wasn't for sure. The pain that was radiating through my skull was nothing compared to the pleasure I was experiencing.

Still holding onto the base of my penis, she released it

from her mouth making a 'pop' sound. She took her tongue and swirled it around my engorged head and wrapped it around the end and sucked as if it were her own personal lollipop. She was teasing me, and I didn't have one single objection against that.

I finally opened my eyes and looked down towards the woman on the floor. I was a bit surprised because it wasn't the blonde haired, blue eyed Tracy that I was expecting, but rather the raven haired temptress with glowing green irises, staring back at me.

Sheridan.

I knew in the back of my head that it was just my mind playing tricks on me, and it was still Tracy on her knees in the bathroom stall, but I didn't care, I was going along with it.

Sifting my hands into her hair and pulling her head towards me, I thrust my hips making my erection hit the back of her throat. I was forcing her to take it all the way. I felt her relax her throat and hum as she continued sucking my dick. She didn't care that I took over the reins, she was a pro at this.

"Play with my balls," I forced out. And instantly she obeyed, cradling both of them in her hand massaging them with just the slightest of pressure.

I felt myself nearing my release and I couldn't be a bastard and not let her get anything in return, so since she had a skirt on, I commanded, "Do you have any panties on?" After the shake of her head stating what I already knew to be true, she knew what she wanted coming to Emmy Lou's tonight, and she didn't need any extra material in her way from achieving that mission. "Hike your skirt up and take a finger and start rubbing your clit."

She blinked several times before her hand released my balls and she followed my instructions. I knew the exact moment when she touched her tiny nub, because she released a groan that had vibrated my dick that was still lodged deep in her throat.

"You like that don't you? You like me telling you what to do?" I said cockily as I began to feel the telltale tingle start at the base of my spine. Still imagining that it was Sheridan taking my cock to such heightened ecstasy, I began pumping harder and faster.

Poor Tracy was being a good sport though, taking my relentless violation like a fucking champ.

"Are you still playing with your pussy?" Once she nodded her head, I told her, "Rub your clit harder and faster, I'm almost there and if you want to get off now too, you'll need to hurry."

She whimpered, which I took to be in the affirmative, as I picked up my speed. Feeling myself on the verge of release, I said, "If you don't want me to cum in your mouth, you need to pull out now." But like the girl that she was, she sucked harder. After her head bobbed just a few more times, I exploded my release inside the depths of her mouth, and she swallowed every drop of it without making a sound. When she was almost done, she started moaning and pumping faster which meant she was finding her own orgasm. Which was just as well, because I was ready to go.

Once she released my dick, I pulled up my boxer briefs and jeans, tucking myself back in place. And I turned and unlocked the stall door and walked towards the sink so I could wash my hands and leave.

Tracy obviously didn't get the memo because she came up behind me, rubbing her hand across my back.

"Tracy, thanks for...that." I said while indicating with a jerk of my head towards the stall we had just inhabited. "But that's all it's ever going to be. Sorry," I said as I shrugged my shoulders and walked out of the men's restroom. I felt like a bastard, but I was sure she knew the score before this even began. I guess she couldn't get it through her thick skull or perhaps it was the ten pounds of makeup that was impenetrable, whichever it was, I wasn't going to stick around and watch her cause a scene.

Turning the corner to head back out into the main portion of the bar, I passed Charlie who has a stupefied look on his face as he blurts out, "Dude...Tracy?" As a look of pure disgust paints his face.

"I know. I know." I muttered as the shame of what just took place began coursing through my veins. I had totally made an ass of myself, and all for what? To get Sheridan out of my head? Well, if I thought it was going to work, I just totally proved myself wrong, because now I wanted her more than anything.

CHAPTER 5

Sheridan

I awoke sometime in the early afternoon, not believing that I actually slept so long, but the clock that sat on the bedside table confirmed it to be true. I couldn't remember the last time I was able to relax into such a deep and restful slumber. It had to have been the fact that I felt safe in Mike's home, even though he wasn't much for company, his home was entirely inviting.

The throbbing of my foot reminded me that it was well past time to take my pain medication. I wasn't one to be thrilled about taking medicine, but I have experienced excruciating pain with no means of medicinal relief, so if the option was there for me, I was going to take it.

I peeled back the covers to the full-sized bed and opened the curtains to the window that was placed to the left of where the bed sat. The sun was shining and the birds were chirping, it was going to be a glorious day.

Since I took a shower last night, after Mike left and after the little incident in the hallway that I would really like to remember, but I didn't really want to discuss. I went ahead and picked out a pair of cutoff shorts and just a red slim-fitting V-neck t-shirt and slipped them on.

I placed my duffel and my keyboard on the bed, so everything would be ready once I called a cab to take me to the nearest hotel until I could find out what I was going to do. Looking at my Yamaha PSRE433 Portable Keyboard, it wasn't as fantastic as my fully restored 1906 Steinway & Sons Model A Grand Piano that was collecting dust in my parents' garage. It was given to me by my late grandmother after I received my acceptance letter to Juilliard right before she passed. It would've killed her to know that I never got the chance to play a single concerto with the Juilliard Orchestra or that I never even made it to the threshold of the front doors to the school.

I let love lead my path for my future. And in the end, all that love did was destroy the things that led to my happiness. Looking down at my hands and curling them into a ball then extending them to where my hand was stretched out, they actually didn't feel half bad today. I was sure that they would ache after playing last night, but I wouldn't overdo it by playing again today. I knew my limits.

I grabbed my brush and ran it through my long, poker straight black hair and secured it with a simple ponytail holder. Most women hated their hair and wished they had the opposite of what they had. Take for example, they had brown curly hair, they wished that they had blonde, straight hair. I was the exception, I absolutely loved my straight black hair. I was lucky that it was completely natural and I had never colored it once in my life. It was long and reached almost to the top of my tailbone, it was the one thing that I truly loved about myself, the one thing that he had never tainted. I slipped on a plain black flip-flop, I needed something that was easy to walk in along with this stupid boot. I was going to see if Mike cared if I had a cup of coffee before I called the local cab company.

Opening the door the guest room, Sadie came charging down the hallway towards me. For a minute, I didn't think she was going to stop before she skidded across the hardwood floors and straight into me. "Sadie, stop!" I yelled a little more aggressively than I intended, but she stopped dead in her tracks and laid down on the floor. *Great, now I've upset his dog.*

I walked closer to where she was stationed and bent down so I could scratch her tummy and give her some lovin'. "Hey there, Sadie. I didn't mean to yell, but I didn't want you to run into my foot." She showed her acceptance of my apology by licking my hand and letting her tail wag a mile a minute. She was such a beautiful and well-behaved dog.

"Where's Mike?" I asked as if she would actually answer my question. "Is he in a better mood today?"

I walked through the living room, the sound of my boot hitting the wooden surface made an echo throughout the house. I would be glad when I was able to get this thing off, even though I had six grueling weeks left ahead of me.

I made it to the kitchen and approached the coffee maker, still without hearing a peep out of Mike. Perhaps, he was sulking in the confines of his bedroom, well that was alright with me. I would get my coffee fix, call the cab company, and write him a note thanking him for letting me stay at his home for one night.

There was almost a full pot of coffee still sitting in the carafe, all I would have to do was reheat it up in the microwave. I would much rather have freshly brewed coffee, but this coffee was better than no coffee at all. After opening up his cabinets, which were neatly organized if I might add, I shuffled through them and found a clean coffee mug. Making it just how I liked it, one sugar and a splash of milk, I was going to make myself comfortable on that wondrous bay window bench.

Seeing a notebook perched up on a bowl on the end of his countertop made me stop my trek across the kitchen. I didn't want to be rude looking through his things, but the way it was situated made me think that it was meant for me.

I sat my mug down beside the notebook and picked the bound papers up in my hands. Reading over the note, I felt a smile spread across my face at his chicken scratch writing and the words that were written.

Sheridan,

I'm working a twenty-four hour shift at the station so I won't be off until around five am tomorrow. Sadie is used to it, so don't worry about her. As long as I don't have a run, I should be able to run by to let her out this evening around seven.

Mike

P.S. I'm sorry for being an asshole last night. Please stay...

I supposed that there was still some goodness lurking around in that man's heart. He wasn't entirely hopeless.

Looking at the clock on the microwave, the green numbers illuminated the time, it was two pm, which meant I still had another five hours before Mike would possibly be home to let Sadie out. He would have no way of knowing whether or not I stayed, so to show my gratitude, I was going to make him dinner.

This would be the first time I made dinner for a man who didn't order me to. I was completely giddy in knowing I would never have to take orders from a man, one man in particular, ever again.

Several hours passed by pretty quickly, but that could've been the fact that I took the opportunity to soak up some sun in that gorgeous backyard of his. I relaxed in the hammock while Sadie laid down below. I was able to imagine living in Brown

County for good, so far, except for my wreck, it had been an extremely quaint and forthcoming little town.

Having a family and making a life here, that sounded like a pretty decent goal and hopefully it would be easily obtainable.

I ended up making something pretty simple, spaghetti. It sounded amazing at the time and it was one thing he had all of the ingredients for. I was extremely pleased with the vast array of spices he had circulating in his cabinet. I was able to add garlic and basil, a staple in any good tomato sauce.

I waited around until seven-thirty before I fixed myself a heaping plate full of al dente spaghetti noodles topped with my homemade tomato sauce and brought it into the living room.

I tucked my right leg underneath my body and rested my boot on the coffee table in front of me. Having my plate rest on my lap, I flipped through the channels on his sixty inch TV until I stopped on one of my favorite sitcoms from the nineties, *Roseanne*. Sadie whimpered from the floor and placed her head on the edge of the couch.

I stuffed myself so completely full that I felt as if I would burst at the seams at any given moment. It was totally welcomed though just to be able to eat as much as I wanted whenever I wanted.

I moved the plate from off of my lap to sit it in the middle of the coffee table and shifted to where I was laying on my side, my boot propped up on the other arm of the couch.

It was eight pm now so I guessed Mike was having a rather busy night. I greatly hoped that his runs weren't anything too terribly horrific or extreme.

Now that my stomach was stupid full, which I almost regretted eating too much, I felt too lazy to do anything else at the moment. I decided that I would rest and watch another episode of *Roseanne* then I would clean up the kitchen and store the leftovers away in the fridge.

Patting my left hand on my side, I called for Sadie to

come up beside me on the couch.

She stood and walked in front of me, taking her time roaming her cold, damp nose over my face as she sniffed making me cower back as it tickled.

"Come on, Sadie," I said again as I patted my leg and made a kissy noise.

Hesitating only a second longer, she leaped up and over my legs and laid down behind me with her head resting on my hip. She sighed with what I would like to think was contentment as I scratched behind her ears.

It took absolutely no time at all before we were both sound asleep.

CHAPTER 6

Mike

Getting off of work this morning, I didn't know what I would be walking into, and the picturesque scene that was before me never even crossed my mind.

It would almost be endearing if Sadie wasn't breaking my one constant rule; no getting on the furniture.

Sadie's head was buried behind Sheridan's back and they were both completely out. And by the looks of it, they've been there for quite a while.

Sadie hadn't even moved a muscle when I came through the front door which was extremely abnormal. Normally she would be standing there at the door waiting for me with her tail wagging back and forth a mile a minute ready to pounce.

Now it seemed she was entirely wrapped up in Sheridan. Traitor.

I decided to leave them laying on the couch while I was able to quickly shower and change out of my uniform.

I really had tried to come home last night because my curiosity was piqued more than anything on whether or not Sheridan had stayed, but it was one run after another, almost nonstop.

After our last call, my partner and I had finally caught a break around midnight and was able to catch a few hours of uninterrupted shut eye until the next shift came on to relieve us.

I was normally able to come home sometime during mid-shift to give Sadie some attention, but it wasn't exactly unheard of if I didn't.

Sadie always had a bowl of kibble and water at her disposal and my back door had a doggy door so she was able to get out in the fenced in backyard to attend to her business.

I took one last glance at Sheridan as she was sleeping peacefully, I've watched her sleep more in the last few days than I've spent with her awake.

"Sadie..." I said in a heavy-handed tone, which seemed to be the common reoccurring theme going on.

Her chocolate brown head quickly perked up as if she had just realized I was there. And all I had to do was cock my brow and she was getting up off of Sheridan and the couch and rushed towards her bed in the dining room with her tail in between her legs.

Little shit knew she wasn't supposed to be up on the couch.

I sat down on the edge of the coffee table and the force of Sadie's moving must have jarred Sheridan awake because the next thing I knew she threw herself into a sitting position on the couch. Her eyes completely bulging out of her head as she shook her head to the sides and then rushed towards the kitchen while repeating, "I'm sorry," over and over again.

Everything happened so fast I didn't exactly comprehend everything at the moment, her skittish actions kind of took me aback. She then rushed into the living room and retrieved her plate that was resting on in the middle of my wooden coffee table, her eyes were completely glassed over as she kept on apologizing. Was she even awake or aware of what was going on?

I decided to let things be for the moment, I didn't want to scare her but I was quickly becoming concerned with what was going on. When I heard the crash of pans on the floor, I knew it was time to take action.

I ran into the kitchen to find the kitchen floor painted in red tomato sauce and Sheridan on her hands and knees picking up strands of dried spaghetti with her fingers.

"Sheridan?" I asked coming up behind her and grabbing her waist and hoisting her up on my granite countertop.

She had yet to answer me and kept staring at the mess on the floor. Her hands were shaking which made her entire body tremble. It was almost like she was someplace else.

"Sheridan?" I asked once again, only to get the exact same response, none.

I spread her legs wide so I could step in between them, at the time I wasn't thinking anything sexual because I was trying to get to the bottom of the situation. But when the inside on her parted thighs came in contact with my stomach and her legs seemed to squeeze in a bit around me, I felt that unfamiliar pull again.

Her hands, which were still covered in spaghetti sauce had calmed down from the relentless shaking and were now resting on her thighs, but she still had yet to look at me.

I cupped my hands on her face and directed it to where she had to see me, but her eyes were still glassed over.

What the hell had happened to her? I thought.

"Sheridan," I said once again, but with an ever so soft tone, I was almost whispering.

She seemed to snap out of whatever trance she was in and those fierce green orbs focused into mine glistening with unshed tears.

By this time, my heart was beating just a bit faster and my breathing, a bit heavier. My thumbs rubbed circles on her cheeks without my brain directing them to.

"What happened, Sheridan?" I didn't want to pry, but there had to be some kind of logical explanation for this.

She looked down at her hands as she turned them over in front of her, noticing the red substance from the discarded tomato sauce. She finally spoke up, "I'm so sorry, Mike. I have arthritis in my hands and sometimes they just forget how to function and drop things." A single tear cascaded down her cheek and I quickly brushed it away.

That solved the problem about the spaghetti mess on my floor, but she didn't emphasize on the apparent trance she had been in.

I was at a loss on what to say or do. Being a paramedic I knew that arthritis could sometimes affect the use of extremities it was settled in, and hearing the level of expertise she had on just a musical keyboard, her fingers could definitely have arthritis in them.

Her eyes continued to linger on mine then she moved to hop off of the counter, but I caught her around her waist so I could set her gently on the floor. She was covered in spaghetti, so she quickly excused herself to the bathroom to wash up, leaving me to clean the kitchen.

I looked over to see Sadie lying on the outskirts of the mess on the floor. I imagined that if she could speak that she would say, 'What was that all about?' the look in her eyes conveyed exactly that.

"Your guess if as good as mine, girl." Don't worry, I haven't lost my mind, at least I didn't think I had. I knew several people who talked to their dogs and imagined them answering you. No? Just me?

That's alright, I rather liked that Sadie couldn't answer me. I didn't have to deal with back talk or smart attitudes.

After cleaning up the mess, in which I had to throw out my mop because it was now stained red, I went ahead and started preparing breakfast.

Sheridan still hadn't emerged from the other end of the house, so I hoped that she was a fan of omelets.

I placed my skillet on the burner closest to me on my right and turned the knob to my electric stove on high, to get the pan nice and heated. Next, I diced up some ham, peppers, and mushrooms into bite-sized pieces and placed them to the side, letting a few 'accidentally' fall to the floor. I was really surprised that Sadie didn't try to gobble up the leftover spaghetti with her vacuum of a muzzle, but she was very quick to snatch the ham off the floor.

Cracking a few eggs into a bowl, I scrambled them up with a fork.

A light "ahem" stopped me during my assault on the eggs.

I casually peeked over my shoulder at Sheridan leaning against the counter and the fork I was holding slipped out of my hand, making a loud clang as the metal from the utensil clattered against my glass bowl.

I had instantly felt my lungs deflate as all of my oxygen left my body.

Sheridan had emerged freshly showered with a haphazard braid cascading over the front of her shoulder. She was dressed pretty casually in a pair of short cut-off shorts, much like what she was wearing earlier, and a black, white, and green striped top which hung off of one shoulder.

The creamy flesh of her shoulder was very enticing and I felt myself longing to wrap my lips around the juncture where her neck and shoulder met.

But that wasn't all, she had done something to her eyes to make them stand out and appear more prominent. Mascara or something, I wasn't one who paid attention to the beauty terms and what not.

And her lips. Those beautiful, tempting, sultry lips were painted a deep crimson.

Red the color of love, lust, and seduction.

Dear God, my resolve was almost non-existent within a day of being around her. She had bewitched me. How did I think this arrangement would be possible?

"Goddess."

Once the word slipped from my lips, I tried my best to think of something to cover up my accidental word oversight.

"Mike?" she asked questioningly as her face morphed into a look of pure confusion.

"Yeah," I said as I quickly recovered grabbing the fork and remembering what I was supposed to be doing at the present time.

"Omelet?" I held up the bowl that contained the eggs and fork.

"Yes, please." She said as her eyes suddenly got wide and she raised a hand to where she was pointing past me to my stove. "But uh, your pan is smoking."

Jesus Christ, if we needed a sign that neither of us should be in the kitchen for *any* reason, we definitely had it.

I quickly moved the scorching pan to the cool back burner and turned the exhaust fan above the stove on high. I hoped it would get rid of the billowing smoke quickly.

I rested a hand on my hip and lightly chuckled. "Contrary to what just occurred, I can cook," I said while cracking a small smile.

I heard Sheridan's breath hitch and I looked back at her and saw she had a bewildered expression on her face.

She went to the cupboard to retrieve two coffee mugs. I had only went as far as to make the coffee, and hadn't even had a cup.

"How do you take your coffee?" she softly spoke to me.

I had resumed my omelet making process and lifting the cutting board up showing what all could be put in the omelets.

She quickly eyed the choices and immediately said,

"Everything in it, please. Oh, but extra mushrooms." She finished a bit sheepishly and I began adding in chopped bits of ham, peppers and fulfilling her request of extra mushrooms.

I guess I was taken aback because Erin never asked or hell even offered to make my coffee. Now that I think of it, she never ever cooked me a meal, and we were married several years. Sheridan cooked dinner for me last night, granted it was left uneaten and ended up covering my kitchen floor, but it was the thought that counts.

Realizing she was still waiting on my answer, I said, "Black, two sugars, please."

Nodding her head, she went to work on my coffee while I kept an eye on her omelet.

Things were kind of awkward between us and I wondered if she was embarrassed about seeing me in all my naked glory. She liked what she saw, she was just trying to cover it up with her smart mouth.

"You seem different this morning."

"Different, how?" I quipped. I began racking my brain trying to think if I was acting any different.

"You seem…happy I guess. Nice even, you even laughed a bit and smiled. It was…nice." Her cheeks turned flushed. She stirred my coffee with a small spoon and tapped off the liquid remnants on the side of my mug before placing it next to me.

I almost started feeling a little nervous at the thought of her being flirtatious with me.

I flipped her omelet over so the underside would cook thoroughly as she again spoke up.

"You must've gotten over your PMS'ing."

I whirled around to see her back to me as she placed the milk back in my fridge.

Sheridan and her smart mouth was going to get her into trouble one of these days.

We each took our plates into the living room and sat

respectively on opposite ends of the couch, making sure there was plenty of room in between us.

She was sending all sorts of mixed signals, so I thought I should stick to my original plan of not wanting anything to do with her.

I reached for the remote off of the coffee table and she ended up snatching it up just a split second before me.

"What do you think you are doing?" I asked in a no nonsense tone. This was *my* house wasn't it? Who did she think she was just stealing my remote and manning the TV?

She continued to sit back on the couch, casually flipping through the on screen guide, trying to find something suitable to her liking I supposed.

Finally ending her perusal on a show that I hadn't watched in years, she tucked the remote underneath her thigh and picked up her fork so she could start digging into her omelet.

"Mmm…this is really good, Mike, thank you."

"Sure, but why are we watching *this*?" I scoffed.

"Are you pouting because we are watching *Roseanne*? I absolutely love this show. And even though it had the most epic ending ever, my favorites are still the early years."

I sat back and began devouring my own omelet and in between taking sips of the coffee Sheridan made. I knew she didn't do anything different to it, and even though I actually brewed the coffee, it still tasted better than any I had ever made.

The episode that was on was a fight between the oldest daughter Becky and Roseanne. I believed that's what most of the episodes consisted of; a fight amongst someone within the family. But like any good sitcom, it was resolved by then end of the thirty minute time slot.

"You know what I like most about this show?" Sheridan spoke in the midst of swallowing a bite, breaking the silence that ensued between us after a few minutes.

"What's that?" Normally it wouldn't matter to me either way whether she answered or not. But I felt almost as if I wanted to get to know her better, what made her tick, what she was afraid of.

She pointed her fork at my TV to accentuate what she was trying to convey. "The fact that they are a regular family, they didn't have much money. Hell half of the time they would call the utility company and tell them some kind of fly by the seat of their pants lie that their check ended up being sent to the cable company. When, in fact, they just didn't have the money to pay for it. But whatever obstacle they faced, they did it as a family. They may not have been your typical All American family, but what I wouldn't have given to be part of the Conner clan."

She sounded almost sad towards the end of her explaining. I wondered if her home life was less than to be desired.

"Did you not have a good life growing up?" I didn't think before I reacted, but I couldn't just sit and stew on it, I needed to know.

"No, nothing like that. I had a fantastic childhood, never lacked for anything. I was an only child and my dad started having heart problems early on, but that has never really stopped him from enjoying life. My mom is absolutely amazing, my best friend, but she is so extremely soft spoken, I don't think I'd ever heard her yell at anyone a day in her life. See the reason why I wished I was part of the Conner family, even though I know they are fictional, it's the fact that Roseanne never took shit from anyone. If a boy didn't treat either of her daughters with anything less than the utmost respect, she effing told them about it. I don't blame my family at all, because overall it was my fault. But if I had been a little less blinded by love and my mom a little more forceful in her actions, then maybe my outcome would've been a whole lot different."

"Well, what about your dad, couldn't he have done

anything?"

"Well, as I said my dad has heart problems, he never really knew the entirety of what went on. I think if he knew even close to the extent of what I've endured, it would kill him. So keeping him secretly in the dark, is what was best."

"I see. And what exactly went on?" I got the impression it had something to do with a guy, but she wasn't being any more forthcoming on her past.

Before she was able to answer, not that she would have anyways, her cell phone rang.

Looking at the screen, she gave me an apologizing glance and answered.

"Hey, Mama," I heard her say. I had finished eating my omelet and was going to take both of our plates into the kitchen.

I overheard her ask how *he* was so I assumed she was talking about her dad since he had heart problems.

Having her talk about her parents made me miss my ma. She passed away six months after her official diagnosis.

That was the worst day of my life. My heart broke for my mother's breast cancer diagnosis, but it was completely obliterated at the loss of my princess.

I braced my hands on the edge of my sink and hung my head down low. Hannah would've been eight soon. It was something that I thought about every day, and even with time the pain never lessened. But for some reason today it got to me a little more. I didn't know if it was the fact that my emotions were running rampant. Sheridan brought out every single emotion, even the ones I had thought that I had buried down deep long ago.

That day was still as fresh in my mind today as if it had happened yesterday. The gut wrenching agony I felt, I changed as a person, honestly what parent wouldn't? I would never have any more kids, I couldn't ever place myself in the position ever again.

Another valid reason to keep my distance from Sheridan, she was young and vibrant, and more than likely would want children. We couldn't ever have anything more than a physical attraction.

My mood had now turned sour, I needed to get out of this house, away from the thoughts of possibly wanting more out of life.

CHAPTER 7

Mike

I pulled in front of Ray's Auto and shut off the engine, I was trying to decide if I wanted to go in or not. It was still early in the day, so Brock would still be working, and he would take one look at me and then the assault of questions would commence.

Brock was really the only friend I had around Brown County, he was the only one I felt comfortable enough confiding in. Yes, he knew about my past, but he was the only one here that did, and I preferred it that way. If he had mentioned it to Tessa, his wife, I didn't know. She had always busted my chops from day one, but that was just the type of person that she was. I had no doubt in my mind that if she knew, things would've changed between us.

I wondered for a brief moment if Sheridan would get along with her, but Tessa made it her mission to get on everyone's good side.

I decided to go ahead and head inside, hopefully Brock would have some work for me to accomplish. Working on vehicles took me back to my roots, it was *home*.

Hopping down from my position in my truck, I carefully closed the door and went into the garage through the open bay door.

Brock was definitely working and by the sounds of what was currently blasting through the speakers, Ray wasn't. Foreigner's "Juke Box Hero" was up almost a few notches too high, but that was how we worked best.

Walking further into the bay, I immediately felt myself relax as the tension left my body. Just the lingering smell of grease and oil, my bad mood was rapidly dissipating. Now let's hope that he had some disassembled car that I could tinker with.

I went to the old Magnavox Shelf Stereo, something that was made probably circa 1990 and turned the volume down by using the control dial. Yeah, no remote for this thing, it even had the Cassette player along with the CD player. But inside a dingy garage, where there was grease literally in every nook and cranny, you didn't want to have some top of the line iPod docking station only to be ruined by a miscalculated thrown wrench when you were aiming for the toolbox. Not that I was speaking out of experience.

"Whoever that is better have a damn good reason for turning down my song during the best part," I heard Brock's muffled words before I saw him as he was laying on a creeper nestled up underneath a newer Ford Fusion. He used his legs to roll himself out from beneath the car and the instant he saw me, the scowl he had on his face disappeared.

"What if I would've been a customer?" I asked. Even though Brock was the manager, Ray still owned the garage and he wouldn't take that shit from anyone even if Brock was his son.

"I knew it was you. I don't know anyone else who has a dopey ass walk. You shuffle your feet or some shit, it can be heard over the stereo, which wasn't *that* loud." He slid back under the car on the creeper, "Why don't you make yourself useful and hand me an Allen wrench."

I walked over to the Industrial Craftsman tool chest and retrieved the tool requested and 'shuffled' my way back, handing him the wrench.

I decided to lean against Sheriff Mitchell's '05 Monte Carlo SS. It wasn't anywhere close to being new and it had some issues, but I absolutely loved its sleek black features.

"So what brings you here?" Brock asked.

"What do you mean? I come here all the time. I was going to see if you needed a hand with anything."

I heard him say, "Hmm," before he pulled himself back out from underneath the car he was working on and raised up into a seated position, resting his arms on his bent knees, spinning the wrench in his hands.

"I know you come here to work and that was my first initial thought that crossed my mind until I saw the guilty look on your face. You may not know or admit it, but you need to talk more than you need to work."

That was just like Brock, he got straight to the point. No beating around the bush.

I lifted my hat up off of my head and brushed my hand over my hair before barely setting it back on my head, the bill pointing towards the sky.

"I just got to thinking about my Ma and then that led to thinking about Hannah. Having Sheridan stay with me is just letting all my pent up emotions run wild."

Brock knew everything there was to know about Erin and Hannah. One night after we had put a restored engine into an old pickup truck, which was a bitch of a task, we cracked open a few beers and then he broke out the tequila. It started being guzzled down freely and the words just started falling out of my mouth. Before I had a chance to reel them back in, the entire story had already been told.

Would I have told Brock my past without the copious

amounts of free flowing alcohol that was coursing through my bloodstream, I couldn't really say one way or the other.

"Ok, let me get this straight. You have an attraction to Sheridan, yes?" I hesitated for only a brief moment before I reluctantly nodded my head. He continued on, "So you don't want to act on that attraction, because..." He shrugged his shoulders, "You feel remorse because of Erin?"

"Remorse for Erin? Absolutely not... Fuck that." I took a defensive stance, "I just can't see myself falling in love with another woman only to be devastated in the most horrendous of ways. And I won't ever have any more children. I refuse to go through that ever again. I don't think my heart could take it."

"Who said you had to fall in love with her?"

He was right, but *Sheridan wasn't a woman who you didn't fall in love with*, I thought to myself.

"Listen," he got up from his spot on the ground, took the grease rag out of his back pocket and began trying to wipe off some of the excess grease, which we both knew was a lost cause.

The tone that his voice took, I knew shit was about to get real.

I crossed my arms in front of my chest as an attempt to brace myself not only mentally but physically for whatever backlash he was about to bestow upon me.

"Ok, here it goes. You and I have been friends for quite a while now right?" He was waiting for visible confirmation, so I lightly nodded my head, urging him to continue and get this over with. "During that entire time, I have *never* seen you happy. You may think you are fooling people into believing that you are, but you don't fool me. Don't you think you deserve to be happy?"

He paused long enough that I thought he was finished, which I supposed was just wishful thinking, because the worst was yet to come.

"Look, I get it man, really I do. If anything ever happened to Blake, I...I don't know what I would do. And just thinking about it, fucks me up, man. But you have been wallowing in your self-guilt for far too long. It wasn't your fault, she was with her *mom*. Albeit, Erin was a poor excuse for a mother, but you didn't know that absolutely no instinct would kick in during the event of a crisis situation. You tried having the world balance on your shoulders and it was too much, you shouldn't have had to do everything alone. A marriage is an equal partnership, most women aren't like Erin. Believe me, if Tessa was, we wouldn't be together. Life is too short to always dwell on the past, I'm not saying forget Hannah, because you will never be able to and you shouldn't. What I am saying is try to move past everything, open yourself up to Sheridan, and get to know her. In the end, it may surprise you and she may be your happily ever after, because Erin sure as hell wasn't. And if anyone would know it would be you, that life is too short. Hannah would want you to live."

He went to retrieve another tool from the tool chest before he went back into his place underneath the Ford Fusion. I sat there in silence for what seemed like forever, really thinking about what he had to say. I did have to balance everything on my shoulders, because if I didn't, absolutely nothing would've gotten done. I was basically the mother and the father in this situation, and I let Erin get away with far too much. But what was to say that the same thing wouldn't have happened if Erin and I weren't together. I'd been to several therapists and it always seemed like a waste of time and money to me, when all along I should've been listening to others around me. I still needed to think about opening myself up to Sheridan, it would be a giant step for me, but one I was leaning towards taking.

I spoke up finally, "When the fuck did we become women, talking about our feelings and shit?" I needed a little humor to lighten up the mood.

He hollered from underneath the car, "I don't know, but don't tell my wife, she would expect me to be in touch with my feelings like this all the time."

CHAPTER 8

Sheridan

I was sitting on the couch with my legs perched up in front of me and my arms wrapped around them when Mike came in. He left in such a hurry earlier, I didn't know if I had said or done something wrong. We seemed to be getting along a little better, but then I had to bring my smart aleck self out. That was something I used to get in trouble by Pate for, but I had managed to keep it in check, and evidently with Mike all bets were off. I couldn't seem to keep my smart ass comments to myself.

Roseanne was still playing on the TV, I was really caught up in the old episodes. It gave me back a sense of life before the railroad collision also known as Pate came into the picture. Sadie immediately ran to his side and I just looked up into his eyes without saying anything at all. I wanted him to have the first word to judge what his mood was like.

"Hey," he breathed out still holding my eyes. He turned to look at the TV, "Still watching this, huh?"

"I'm addicted now, and plus there wasn't anything else on to watch," not that I really took the time to look, but he didn't need to know that.

Cue the awkward silence.

He perked up and snapped his fingers, "I just talked to my buddy Brock down at the garage I work at. He said that Sheriff Mitchell is wanting to sell his 2005 Chevy Monte Carlo, he's trying to get everything situated around here so he and his wife can move up to Virginia to help out his sick sister in law. It now needs a new transmission and a few other minor things, but I think it would probably be easier if I rebuilt it, not to mention much cheaper. Have you talked to the insurance company yet?"

Cue my dumbfounded expression.

"Why are you being so nice to me?" I didn't mean to speak out what I was thinking, but it was too late to take it back now.

He crossed his arms over his chest and widened his stance, which made my lady parts scream with lust. By him standing like that, it made his muscles in his forearms protrude out, and I was ready to beg for him to wrap those meaty arms around me as he has done before.

Where the hell was all this coming from?

He leaned an ear forward, "I'm sorry?" It wasn't an apology, he was wanting me to further explain.

I kind of shrank back into the couch before I began explaining, "I just… You don't know me *at all* and here you are looking for a new vehicle for me, offering me to stay in your house, eating your food," I pointed towards the TV, "watching your TV Sometimes you act like you'd rather I not be here at all and other times you are just so nice to me, I was just wondering why."

I explained my reasoning as best as I could and I hoped he understood where I was coming from.

He uncrossed his arms from where they were perched on his rock hard chest and continued to glare at me. Apparently I didn't say the right thing and he was pissed, I could see the fire flaring in his eyes from my spot on the couch several feet away from him.

"You know what, stay here as long as you need to, but stay the fuck out of my way. Who are you to question why I'm trying to be hospitable, the least you could say is thank you."

And with his parting words he stormed off out of the living room and went towards the kitchen. "Sadie, come!" he screamed. Then mere seconds later I heard the back door slam.

What do I do now?

I didn't mean for him to take offense, I just wanted to know why he was being so nice to me because many people in recent years hadn't. I'd forgotten what it was like to have decent human beings in my life aside from my parents of course.

I felt the tears begin welling in my eyes as I was just basically scolded like a misbehaving child. I thought I had gotten away from feeling like this. I would stay because I really needed to watch my money and I still hadn't called the insurance company; that would be the first thing on my to-do list for tomorrow.

I would somehow show Mike how gracious I was for him letting me stay here. He wouldn't have to lift a finger while he was at home to cook or clean, but I would respect his wishes in staying pretty much out of sight.

CHAPTER 9

Mike

It was a cool and dreary day, the sun had ceased to exist. It looked like at any moment the sky would open up and soak everything in a torrential downpour.

Mother Nature was pretty much matching my mood as of late. I was in a total funk and didn't know the first thing about how to get out of it.

Sheridan did what I reluctantly said and stayed out of my way for the most part. We passed each other going to the bathroom every so often, but she wouldn't even look at me. I was worn out from working all the time, I put in extra hours at the station and when I wasn't there, I was drowning myself in vehicle parts, just to keep out of sight.

I honestly didn't know how to fix whatever 'relationship' we had and I was actually surprised that she was sticking around.

I walked into the garage only to roll my eyes at the odd song choice for Brock to be listening to blaring from the speakers. I didn't want to be bothered, so I just left the volume where it was, even if it was "Can't Touch This" by MC

Hammer.

I grabbed a slightly used shop rag, which meant it didn't have as much grease caked on it as the others, and shoved it into my back pocket. You never knew what would occur being underneath the hood of a vehicle. And I walked over to Sheridan's car which had pretty much taken up residence in a bay within the garage.

She had finally received the insurance check, which was more than what the car was being sold for. So in the end she'll have money left over out of the deal. She'd been leaving money on my kitchen counter for when I went grocery shopping, but I never used it. I invited her to stay at my house, I wasn't about to make her pay for anything.

I remembered back to a few weeks ago when I brought her here to take a look at the car. I knew it was in pretty great condition for the price excluding the fact that it needed a new transmission and odds and ends such as brakes, and a new set of windshield wipers.

That was also the day when she met Brock.

He was piddling around in the backroom where the extra common parts were stored. Oil filters, oil, spark plugs, belts, things like that.

Thinking he was sneaky, he went to the stereo and turned on God knows what and came up beside me.

Sheridan had yet to say anything, she was just walking around the Monte Carlo running a finger alongside the sleek black exterior.

Finally, the stereo kicked on and I inwardly groaned and gave Brock the stink eye as "Do You Wanna Touch Me" by Joan Jett began streaming through the speakers.

I casually glanced over to Sheridan who had a deer in the headlights look and her face quickly flushed, and then looked back at Brock who had the cheesiest fucking grin plastered on his face.

I mouthed the word, "Bastard," to him before he spoke up.

"Pretty nice, huh?" he asked as indicated towards the car. He casually stepped closer in Sheridan's direction wiping his hand on his grease stained dark denim jeans and then held it out for her to shake. "I'm Brock Monroe, it's nice to meet you Sheridan."

She idly took one look at his rough, filthy, overworked hands and I'll be damned if she didn't grasp his hand in a firm handshake.

This woman wasn't afraid to get dirty, she surprised me at every turn.

"It's so nice to meet you as well, Brock. Um, one question," her hand left Brock's as she pointed towards the car, "that's a two door car."

Brock grasped his chin and he partially turned towards me and we each let out a little chuckle. Sheridan wasn't talking to me, but I was the one who answered.

"Yeah, that's right. Monte Carlo's only come in two doors."

"Is that a problem?" Brock asked.

She looked at it a little more before shaking her head no.

Shoving his hands in his pockets, Brock started walking around the car. "This car does need some work, but like I'm sure Mike has told you that he is planning on doing most of the work himself, so it'll keep the costs lower. If you look inside of it, it's in immaculate condition, the mileage isn't bad for the year. Really, you won't find a better deal. It just so happened that Sheriff Mitchell brought it in here and wanted me to help him pass word around that he was selling it. I think it'll be a great car for you, Sheridan."

It looked as if she was mulling over the information that Brock had just given her, which was more or less the same exact thing I had told her before.

"Ok, this will work. Thank you, both of you." I was
honestly shocked that she would thank me, maybe things
wouldn't be so hard to repair after all. She turned around and
went straight back to my truck and climbed in.

She wouldn't let me help her in anymore. No matter if it
was uncomfortable climbing into the truck with a broken ankle,
she was doing it herself. The days of the idle touches were now
just a distant memory.

"Hey man, what's going on?"Brock spoke, which pulled
me from my memory of the weeks prior.

"Oh, hey. Just thought I'd come and work on the tranny a
bit since I had some free time."

I could've honestly had more of it accomplished, but I
was pussy footing around. I didn't want Sheridan to not have to
be dependent on me anymore, not that she asked much of me
anyways.

If her car were up and running, then she could leave
Brown County, and I wasn't ready for that to happen yet, if at
all.

He came out from around the Dodge Durango that he was
working on.

"Is that Ethan Bradley's?" Ethan was a Sheriff Deputy for
Brown County, all around good guy.

"Yeah, his air conditioner was acting up, just needed a
charge really. He wanted me to go ahead and change the oil in it
and rotate the tires since it was already in here, easy stuff."

I nodded my head just to show him that I was partially
listening at least.

"Hey, how are things going at home with Sheridan? Y'all
still tip-toeing around each other?"

"Yeah, I really fucked up. Things are strained at best. I
honestly don't know how to fix them."

"I don't think she was trying to come off as rude, she
really doesn't strike me as the type. Now, is she someone to give

you hell and bust your balls, absolutely, but I don't think her demeanor meant being disrespectful. Perhaps she's just cautious. I mean really she is right, y'all don't know each other, and maybe these feelings of attraction are new for her. I think she's been burned just like you and isn't used to people being nice to her."

I was perpetually dumfounded, he sounded as if he had personally spoken with her.

"How do you know all of this? You speak as if you've had a private conversation with her. Her attraction towards me? I'm fucking lost." I said as I let out a long drawn out sigh and rested my hands on my hips.

"When y'all were here just a few weeks ago, I did talk to her, dumbass. When you went to the bathroom, I went out to the truck and talked to her. I didn't want her sitting in the truck all by herself."

"That couldn't have been more than a few minutes, what all did you get out of her?" I was intrigued. He knew her for all of five minutes and he knew more apparently than I did. Granted, I only knew her about ten minutes longer.

"Not much, and what I did get I'm not repeating. You'll get her full story when you earn it. So stop being an asshole and earn it. How is her foot doing?"

I shrugged my shoulders, because really his guess was as good as mine. "Fine I guess. She is cleaning and cooking nonstop. I haven't had to lift a finger at home since she's been there. I'm sure she needs to take it easy, but since she isn't working, and I'm not accepting any money, she wants to help in her own way. She is an amazing cook, my God. Half the time I am reheating up the meal she makes because there is really no rhyme or reason to what time I come in the door, and usually it's late enough to where I eat and then head to bed. But even reheating it, it's the best things I've ever eaten.

"Oh and get this, I was out on the patio the other morning,

she came out to make coffee for herself, and made mine too. It kind of astounded me, because Erin never ever took the initiative to make me coffee. Sheridan had made me coffee one time before and she'd remembered how I took it. Never mind it's easy as hell to make, but the fact that she took the time to commit it to her memory bank." I stopped talking because I was rambling like a fucking woman. "Oh my God, I've fucking lost my mind. Over a girl, I don't even know. Over someone who isn't even speaking to me at the moment!"

I felt a sharp sting on my face as I then realized Brock's hand connected with my cheek.

"Get a fucking grip, man!" he yelled in my face.

I shook the fogginess out of my head as I stared deadpan at him, "Did you just fucking slap me? You couldn't even punch me, you had to *slap* me?"

"Well, would you like for me to punch you? Because I'm sure that can be arranged. Damn man, you need a good night's sleep."

"Oh, that's another thing. I get woken up every night by Sheridan thrashing around. I think she's having nightmares. The spare bedroom is right next to mine and I can hear her."

This time I got to feel Brock's protruding knuckles as they dug deep into my collarbone as he punched me.

Wincing and bringing my hand to my shoulder, I yelled, "God damn, what was *that* for."

"You deserved it. You said that you can hear her being woken up in the middle of the night by possible nightmares, but yet you aren't doing anything about it? What the fuck is wrong with you? If I didn't know any better, I'd say you were turning into a bonafide pussy. You pretty much said yourself that you were looking for a sign to be able to approach her again, hello, *here is your sign*!!! Go comfort her whenever she has a nightmare, maybe then she'll open up to you and y'all can stop all of this pussy footing around."

He turned around and walked away mumbling something about "Y'all are downright a bunch of fucking teenagers." And, "I'm getting too old for this shit." Then he stopped short and turned around, "I almost forgot to tell you, Emmalynne had her baby yesterday, it was a girl." My heart immediately sank. "I don't suppose you want to go meet Charlotte, do you?"

I knew he could convey my sadness through the perplexed look in my eyes because he gave me a weak smile while nodding his head and said, "I didn't figure so, but I thought you'd like to know."

Emmalynne and Grady were friends, not close friends, so I guess they were more like acquaintances. So even though I wouldn't make an effort to go see them, because being around children is a hard limit for me, I would send them at least a card to let them know that I was thinking about them.

My head was so garbled with so much despair. Who knew that it would take this long for old wounds to heal? Inadequacy in being a man, that's what I felt like. I needed to take a giant step in overcoming my fears about love and about letting someone else in. Brock was right, Hannah would want me to live. So I would try my best and live, for her.

Coming home at night once again, but not because I was stalling because of being afraid of actually holding a conversation with Sheridan, oh how I wished it was.

Walking in through the front door, I helped guide the screen door shut so it wouldn't make a loud clang and end up waking up Sheridan or Sadie.

Today was emotionally and mentally draining. After the turn of events that occurred today, everything was suddenly brought into perspective.

Maggie Walker was kidnapped this morning by some psychotic drug lord who was trying to get to Maggie's brother Mason, and Maggie's boyfriend Charlie Hennings.

Finding out that Charlie was undercover FBI, almost made you feel a little violated. He had been working under the pretense of being a bartender at Emmy Lou's Bar, where I frequented pretty often. I couldn't honestly say that I *knew* him well, but we did play in The Nation's Capital together, him being the bass player.

Luckily Maggie would be alright, and Charlie ended up being shot in the side, but it was only a flesh wound. And the kidnapper met his demise, with several rounds of bullets puncturing his skin. That scene made me glad that I wasn't a coroner.

Being in the back of the ambulance with an unconscious Maggie, made me realize that I was exactly where I should be in life, being a paramedic. I loved being able to save lives, even though I wasn't able to save the ones closest to me. And if that didn't strike me in the heart.

I dropped my lunchbox and gym bag directly on the floor, not even caring where it went. I was in almost a zombie-like state as I walked into the kitchen to no doubt find something that Sheridan cooked and put her heart and soul into because that was just what she did.

She took care of me even if she didn't directly realize it.

I devoured the most succulent bacon wrapped pork tenderloin before I crawled under my sheets for what would be a night of little to no or restless sleep.

That was until I heard the high-pitched shrills of Sheridan yelling, "No Pate, stop!"

CHAPTER 10

Sheridan

Oh no, he had found me. How in the world had Pate found me, here in this Podunk town of all places?

I tried to run away, but the boot that was enclosed around my foot prevented me from moving around very fast.

I could hear the rustling of the leaves as his widely spaced footsteps came quickly approaching. I had no idea how or why I was out in the woods, it was something straight out of a horror movie, which sounded like the last several years of my life.

I thought I had gotten away from him.

I ended up tripping over a large branch that was growing up from the ground, landing flat on my face. My foot was throbbing so profusely that I couldn't even regain the strength to get back to my feet again.

Hearing his heavy, labored breathing getting even closer, I had to think of something to do. Fighting back never stopped him, so what made me think that it would now.

"No Pate, no!" I screamed, hoping he would gain even an ounce of compassion.

I looked over my shoulder only to see his hand coming

closer to me. I squeezed my eyes tightly shut and strained myself into locking my muscles and joints, to try and brace myself for the impact only to feel myself being shook by my shoulders.

"Wake up, Sheridan. You're having another nightmare. Sheridan, sweetheart, please wake up."

That soothing almost trembling voice wasn't the voice of the monstrous Pate. It was the one voice that I longed to hear day in and day out, but hadn't in several days.

Mike.

My eyes immediately flew open as I jerked up in bed, Mike had to abruptly dodge his entire body back, because the impact from our heads colliding would've been excruciatingly painful.

"Whoa, Sheridan it's just me." He calmly stated as he put his hands up in mock surrender. I supposed he thought I was going to attack him. Actually, it was the opposite as I lunged for him thrusting my arms around his neck as I clung to his body.

I was safe in Brown County. No Pate in sight. Nothing to worry about. These nightmares kept getting worse and more and more realistic.

I felt his hand linger on my back as he embraced me and rubbed his fingertips up and down along my spine.

"Shh. It's alright. Nothing can hurt you while you are here with me, do you understand?"

I still didn't trust my voice so I just nodded knowing that indeed I was safe with Mike. And even safer in his arms.

I finally let go of him and settled back onto the mattress, and started feeling a little silly for my freak out.

"I'm so sorry, Mike, I didn't mean to wake you up. I sometimes get bad dreams, it's no big deal."

"One you didn't wake me and two, I've heard that excuse before, and it's time to come up with a new one. And perhaps maybe one a little more believable if you are wanting me to back off. Now, you screamed 'No, Pate' just like last time. Are you ready to tell me who Pate is?"

I hesitated, was I ready to tell him about the *illustrious* Pate Strickland? Illustrious being said with very stern sarcasm. In his everyday professional life, he was highly respected and looked up to because of his father. Within the outer four walls of our house, he was anything but.

He directed me to sit against the headboard as he sat right beside me and covered our lower extremities with a blanket. He turned towards me brushing back some of my hair off of my shoulder. I didn't know why he did that, but the touching movement sent electric zings straight to my heart.

"Sheridan, I'm here to listen, if you are willing to open up."

I again, couldn't find my words and it was beyond frustrating. I didn't know why I was bottled up so tightly. So many concerns were floating around. Would he judge me? Would he think I brought all of this on myself?

Just when I thought that I could convey my fears and insecurities, he took a deep breath and let his words hang in the air, "I was married before."

This surprised me so I swung my head around to where I was looking at him, deep into his eyes. I could see his broken heart right before me.

Instinctively, I reached for his hand and mingled our fingers together and it warmed me that he squeezed my hand back instead of letting it go. He had a story to tell as well, he just started his before mine, and now I was urging him to continue on. I knew that this wouldn't be easy for either of us. Tonight was a turning point in this dance between us, I could feel it deep down to the depths of my soul.

"Erin and I went to school together and began dating in high school. Things were serious and now that I look back on it now, more serious than they should've been. We were just kids for Christ sake. We were twenty-one and had just barely started our actual life when she said that she was pregnant. So, I knew my responsibilities and wouldn't ever slack on them, so we got married, and several months later Hannah was born…"

With the tone in his story, I knew it wasn't going to have a pleasant outcome, but little did I know how extremely devastating this would be.

I could already feel the tears beginning to well up in the corners of my eyes. He would never truly know how deeply he impacted me with his words.

"Erin was a manic depressive and didn't follow her doctor's strict guidelines and medication, so she was lazy, and disconnected from the entire world, and didn't see the wrongfulness in her actions."

I squeezed his hand tighter to silently convey that I was still with him, even though inside I was reeling.

His eyes started to haze over, he was projected right back into that time in his life as he continued on, "Hannah was my entire world, my princess. She hung the freaking moon, I never knew how I could love another human being so much, but I loved that little girl more than anything in this entire world. Erin had goaded me into putting Hannah in preschool whenever she turned three, and I agreed. I thought it would be great for her to interact with other kids her age, make new friends, and learn things that I couldn't teach her, her mom's reasoning for wanting her to go to school, were selfish. Erin just wanted time to herself without having to watch her.

"I worked for my dad, I was the head mechanic at Jameson Auto; I didn't always want to be a paramedic. I was a born and bred mechanic and I enjoyed it, and to an extent I still do. But that Monday morning I had to open the shop because my dad had to take my ma to a doctor's appointment. That was the day my mother was diagnosed with Stage IV Breast Cancer and she ended up losing her battle exactly six months later, but I think a broken heart helped in that matter as well." He wiped a stray tear from his eye, "Sorry I'm getting off track. So because I had to open the shop early I wasn't able to take Hannah to school. Erin wasn't exactly thrilled about it, and I remembered her being hateful and pissed off that she had to get up out of bed to take her own daughter to school.

"The day had went on, but I was constantly on edge waiting to hear the news from my parents. I had to even stop what I was doing to call Erin to remind her to pick up Hannah. Well, a little later I received a phone call from Hannah's school stating that she was struck by a motorist walking across the crosswalk in front of her preschool and that they had just gotten off of the phone with 9-1-1."

My heart lodged in my throat and the onslaught of tears was steadily streaming down my face by this point. I wanted him to stop, needed him to halt his storytelling because I ultimately knew what the outcome would be, but he didn't, he trudged on.

"I don't even remember leaving the garage, I had left all of the doors open and unlocked, I didn't care, and by the grace of God I made it to the scene. I arrived ten minutes after the school had called me, and would you fucking know it that the ambulance didn't pull up until thirty seconds after me. I had rushed over to where the director of her school was holding my little princess," his voice choked up and it became difficult to understand him because he was almost to the point of sobbing. "The director later told me that Hannah was alive when she brought her in her lap and had died while waiting for the ambulance to arrive."

He buried his head in his hands and I could feel the sobs wracking his entire body as I rested my cheek on his shoulder. My heart broke for him and for Hannah. I was speechless, I didn't know what to say or do. I knew better than to give him pity or be overly sympathetic because if he was anything like me, if would just cause more harm than good.

He lifted his head up and sniffed trying to clear out his nose and proceeded even further, "Twelve minutes. It took the ambulance crew twelve fucking minutes to get to my baby girl. In that moment, I knew that I had to become a paramedic because I couldn't let innocent people die in the fucking street because they had to wait twelve fucking minutes for someone to arrive."

"Did Erin get hit as well?" He hadn't said anything further about Erin so I wondered if she was injured or worse.

He let out a maniacal cackle, "Erin didn't get a fucking scratch or a droplet of blood on her. The director of the preschool was covered in Hannah's blood trying to keep my princess alive while Erin stood on the sidewalk and fucking watched. Come to find out, she was walking ahead of Hannah at the crosswalk, not even holding her hand. I sometimes wondered if Erin ever had a motherly bone in her body. That day I lost my Hannah, I lost all respect for that bitch, Erin. I never ever thought I could be the type of person to hate someone, but I loathe that woman with every fiber that I am. For her to just stand there and watch her own daughter die without trying to do a damn thing, that's fucked up."

I was utterly appalled at Erin's actions and I didn't even know the woman. How could any mother not protect her child? I would fight tooth and nail for my child and ultimately to the death to protect them. I was more angered than I had ever been and if Erin were right in front of me, I would have a few choice words to say to her followed by one hell of a beating.

"So the day I buried my Hannah, Erin was served with divorce papers. I've never seen or heard from her since. I went into a pretty deep depression myself and cut ties from everyone including my parents. I quit going into work and began drowning myself in alcohol. It wasn't until the phone call from my dad saying that my mother had died six months later did I finally realize that I needed to get my life together. The day after my ma's funeral I packed up and left St. Louis and haven't been back since. I call my dad on the rare occasion. But I'm different now, things are different. I know my dad suffered through all of this too, but I just can't bring myself to go back there."

I finally spoke up, "How long ago has this all been?"

"Four years."

To think that Mike would've had a seven year old running around. No wonder he kept himself closed up and to himself. I couldn't even fathom what he'd been through and it makes like all of my problems seem like child's play.

He got up from off of my bed and walked out of the room, I didn't hear his door shut, so I assumed he went into the living room.

I was going to give him a few minutes before I went in there to rehash my past. He was brave enough to tell me about the agonizing way he lost his precious princess, that the least I could do was speak up about mine.

I recalled the conversation I had with Brock the other day at the garage, I thought it was strange that he came to the truck while Mike was still inside, but now his words made sense. He told me to be patient with him and not give up because he had been through so much in his entire life. Things were starting to make sense now as to why Mike had been almost guarded with me, he didn't want to open himself up in fear that he would possibly be happy. He felt as if he shouldn't be happy in life and that is the wrong way of going about it.

After fifteen minutes had passed, I walked into the living room to find Mike leaning his head against the back of the couch. I sat down right next to him and rested my head on his shoulder and automatically felt his hand come around and grip mine.

"First, I want to say thank you for trusting me enough with your story. I'm not going to dwell on it, because that wouldn't be what I would want, but I want you to know for what it's worth, I'm sure you were an amazing father, like you should be. And Hannah would be so very proud of you for becoming a paramedic and helping save lives."

"Thank you for that. It feels oddly comforting getting it all out. Brock is the only person in Brown County to really know anything about me."

"Did you love her? Erin I mean." I had no clue why I just asked that question. It was really none of my business.

"Did I love Erin? That is a tough question to answer. At one point in time I believed that I was in love with her, but now I see it as it was infatuation. I think I loved the idea of Erin, but in the end I wasn't really *in love* with her."

He sat there for a moment, before he said something that made my world tilt on its axis, much like the man did himself.

"I do know that I never want any more kids. I don't think I could ever take being subjected to something like that again. Is that selfish of me? Possibly, but if anyone wants to judge me for that, then they really don't know what it's like to lose a child."

"I do."

Two little words were all I could get out. Because I knew what it felt like to lose a child, granted mine was still in utero, but nevertheless I've dealt with that pain.

He turned towards me with a perplexed look on his face, "You do?"

I nodded my head before I started along on my journey through the past.

"Let me start at the very beginning... I was what you more or less would call a child prodigy. I was classically trained and mastered the piano by the age of ten. My childhood consisted of hours upon hours of rehearsing and learning different concertos on the piano, and recitals near and far on the weekends. I was accepted into Julliard with the hopes of achieving a double major, one for concert piano and the other for singing."

I looked down at my damaged hands, although to the average person on the outside they looked like normal hands.

"You sing?" He interrupted my thoughts by that one question.

"Not anymore. I'm sorry, but you will probably never hear me sing, I just *don't* anymore. I still enjoy playing the piano, but sometimes it's just hard for me to because of my arthritis in my hands and fingers.

"Anyways, back to where I was. I was so genuinely thrilled to be one of the ones chosen to study at Juilliard. I wanted to play for the New York Symphony. To have the distinguished honor to play in the Symphony Orchestra in front of all of New York, it was my dream. And it was almost obtainable.

"But fresh out of high school I met Pate Strickland. My story started out much like yours, a lot like yours in fact. It was a whirlwind romance and I really did believe that we were in love. I ended up pregnant shortly after we met so being only eighteen, I cancelled on my dreams so we could follow Pate's. We moved in together and things ended up changing.

"Pate went to school to become a lawyer and in the end he did. You see Pate Strickland's dad is a prestigious judge, so Pate always had a job working with him. Several months into the pregnancy I had some intense abdominal cramping and wanted to go to the hospital to get it checked out. Pate wouldn't let me, he actually refused. We ended up in an argument and he punched me in the stomach. I remembered blacking out and the next thing I knew I woke up in the hospital and had lost the baby. Pate told the doctor's that I fell."

Bringing back all these memories was hell on my tear ducts. I was already covered in tears and my shirt was wet from constantly wiping my eyes on it.

"Being who he was, no one ever even questioned him. He

apologized profusely and promised me that it would never happen again. And I was naïve enough to believe him. Law school was tough on him, stressed him out so he ended up turning to alcohol. You will never *ever* see me drink because I know what it can do to a person. He turned into a hateful, vile person, but I was stuck because of some kind of hold he had over me. He treated me like a slave and forbid me to work. I had to cater to his every whim and cook and clean. I remember the first time that dinner wasn't on the table when he got home from work. He took my only dream left and crushed it, quite literally. When I *misbehaved,* he would break my fingers. I couldn't actually tell you how many times they've each been broken. So much that arthritis has taken over. I do have more good days than bad, but if I spend too much time playing piano I pay for it the next day."

I could see Mike's hands clenched and I covered my outstretched hand over his, to try to get him to ease up the tension.

"It's not worth it," I shook my head as I said, "I'm fine now. When things would get out of hand and he hurt me worse than he anticipated he would bring me to the hospital, but he would tell everyone that I was clumsy. Who would believe me over him? No one that's who, I tried profusely to tell someone when we went, but no one listened to me. It got to the point to where he would lock me in the house and I wasn't able to leave at all. I was a prisoner in my own home. The majority of the time he forced me to have sex with him, no matter the time or the place, when he wanted it, he got it. I lived outside my own head for those sessions, because if I hadn't I clearly wouldn't have been sane."

CHAPTER 11

Mike

Listening to Sheridan rehash her past was tearing me up inside. She was forced to basically give up everything and live inside of some morbid prison. And to think no one would listen to her cry for help because of his father? I was completely infuriated that some man thought he could treat someone that he supposedly loved like this. I wished I knew where exactly this Pate Strickland was, but that was the thing, Sheridan never divulged where she was from.

I felt that new familiar pull when she wrapped her hand around mine to try to ease my tension. I could feel my blood pressure skyrocket just by listening to her.

"I managed to get away once before now. It was a little over three years ago, he was running late for an important exam and forgot to set the alarm." She must've registered my surprised reaction when I raised a brow. "Yeah, that's the funny thing, most people had alarms for keeping people out; this alarm was for keeping me in.

"I ran to my parents and skimmed over most of the situation and was able to stay off of his radar for eleven months.

Eleven wonderful months."

She seemed to get a twinkle in her eye, I could tell that the time away from him was good for her. But then I thought about her living here. She never goes out, she cooks and cleans for me. And even though I didn't know any better, I was no better than Pate, keeping her hoisted inside of the house. I would have to make it my mission to take her out, see more of Brown County.

"What happened after the eleven months?"

"He found me. My parents had moved during that time I was home and tried to keep everything conspicuous, but the one time I go to the store, he finds me. He told me that if I didn't come with him that he would find my family and kill them. So what choice did I have? I was his puppet again to do as he pleased. Until that one fateful day about three months ago, I left for good. I don't know if he is searching for me, but he had been eyes deep in cases at the law firm, so I suspect he wouldn't have even had the time. I stopped at my parents for a week, got my last name changed, got my old car that luckily still ran and went on my way in finding somewhere new to start my life over. And low and behold, I get in a wreck in a small ass town and met someone who I hope will become a great friend, if we can get over each other's insecurities."

She nudged her shoulder into mine, which caused me to look into her eyes, she was talking about me, she wanted to be friends. That was just my luck, here I finally decided that I wanted to try and have more with this woman, she decides to throw out the friend card. But I would take whatever I could get.

"I'm sorry all that happened to you, Sheridan. Really I am, and here I've been awful to you. No more cooking or cleaning while you're here, got it?" I said and I really wasn't joking.

"Oh, you don't have to worry about that, I actually like cooking. And I like it even more when I'm not being forced."

I laid my head back on the couch again, I was absolutely exhausted. So much raw emotion floating around today. It had been one fucking long ass day and I was ready for a new day with hopefully a lot more laughs and a lot fewer tears.

The next thing I knew, Sadie was nudging my knee and when I looked up, the sunlight was pouring in through the curtains. Stretching out an arm, I realized that my other one was asleep, but it was because Sheridan was curled up next to me on the couch wrapped around it. I felt the hint of a smile flit across my face as I so gently tried to remove my arm from her sleepy clutch without waking her up.

It was a failed attempt as she started stretching as well, but pushing her chest out, accentuating her mouthwatering breasts. It didn't help that I currently had morning wood, and this was just too enticing not to watch.

I kept staring until she let out a yawn and a sleep-filled, "Good morning. I do have to say Mr. Jameson that you make an amazing pillow and I ended up sleeping great. But that could also be the fact that I was completely drained."

"I agree. I slept very well even though this couch doesn't normally sleep the best. Um, I do have a question about last night if that's alright."

Something had been niggling in the back of my mind.

"Um, ok."

"Last night you said that he doesn't know where you are and that you don't think he's coming for you, but what if he is? And your real last name isn't Nichols?"

"Technically, that was two questions, but in the light of the matter I'll let it slide."

She tried to joke, but it really just made me want to shut her up by kissing her smart ass mouth.

"For all intents and purposes, my last name is now Nichols. And, yes, Pate could be looking for me. But honestly, I'm free now, I can't live my life in constant fear. I'm six hours away from him, and with my last name different, I think it would be a little harder for him to find me. But I would rather not talk about this anymore, it's the past. I'm going to be trying to make a new life for myself and if Brown County is going to be it, I need to start looking for a job."

I was reluctant to let her explanation go, but I would definitely be on the lookout. I could possibly let the Sheriff's department know to be on the lookout as well.

And I was extremely excited to even hope that she would stay in Brown County permanently.

She put her booted foot on the coffee table and stretched again.

"Oh, I forgot to tell you, I had my Doctor's appointment yesterday and apparently I've been doing too much on my feet and haven't been resting enough, so I'm stuck in the boot for another four weeks. I'm just ready to get this damn thing off." She said as leaned forward to try and readjust the boot.

I was surprised to hear that she had her appointment. How in the world did she get there?

"Why didn't you tell me about your appointment? How did you get there?"

She scoffed a little before I could tell that her smart aleck self was about to make a reappearance.

"I'm telling you now, and I took a cab. I knew you had to work and have been working a lot lately, so I didn't want to bother you with my appointment."

Well, when she put it that way...

We were now finally underway into the summer months as it was closing in on the end of June. Things were pretty amazing if I did say so myself, which obviously I did.

I admit that Sheridan and I still tiptoe around the obvious attractions we have for one another, but I could sincerely call her my best friend.

I never thought I would identify with someone so well, we complement each other perfectly.

We went yesterday to get her cast taken off and I never thought that I would see someone so excited to be able to wear two normal shoes. The first thing she wanted to do was go get a pedicure and she made me endure one with her. Although I would deny this to my grave, it actually felt amazing.

I drew the line at a manicure. If Brock would've taken one look at my nails and saw my cuticles cut down and clean nail beds, I don't think I would've heard the end of it.

I actually found myself wanting to be home with her rather than working. I still worked my normal paramedic shifts, but I didn't go to the garage as much, which meant that Sheridan's car was really no closer to being finished.

She really didn't seem to mind though, we laughed and carried on all the time, and we've even taken to making dinner together. And yes, we still watched *Roseanne* pretty regularly. And she was in fact right, being in the Conner family would've been pretty awesome, there definitely wouldn't have a lack of hilariousness.

To the average person looking in, you would see that I was, in fact, happy for the first time in a long time. I was just missing that one special piece of Sheridan that I truly wanted; her heart. I'll be a man and admit that I was already halfway in love with her and what I wouldn't give to make her truly mine.

But there was absolutely nothing that I could do about it, she had pulled out that friend card over a month ago and I would take what I could get. She was etched so deeply into my heart that I couldn't risk losing her by taking this further.

Sadie brought me out of my reverie by placing her tennis ball by my leg and nudging her cool, wet nose on my hand.

It was such a beautiful day out, so Sadie and I were playing fetch outside. Well, Sadie was doing the fetching while I sat on the patio.

It had rained all day yesterday, so an idea sparked in my head as something fun to do. And I could almost bet that Sheridan had never done it before.

Speaking of the goddess, Sheridan came outside dressed in yet another pair of cutoff shorts that accentuated those long, lean legs and a racer back tank top. Today her hair was piled on top of her head, she had already been complaining of the heat with her long ass hair, but refused to cut it. I silently thanked God that she did. She handed me a glass full of iced tea before she sat down beside me.

I took a long gulp, it tasted so refreshing. Sheridan really knew how to make the perfect sweet tea.

"Thank you that hit the spot."

"You are very welcome." She took a drink out of her own glass and sat it down on the patio table. "You know what? I want to do something fun today. I mean I just finally got my cast off and I think we just need to go have an adventure or something."

Could she read my mind or what?

"Well, I actually just had an idea for something fun to do myself. I'm sure that it's something that you've never done before and as long as you aren't opposed to getting a little dirty, I think we would have one hell of a time."

CHAPTER 12

Sheridan

"We are doing *what*?" I screeched once we pulled up in front of an old style brick ranch home that was absolutely gorgeous and had a scenic lake basically in its front yard. It was complete with a dock that sat two hunter green Adirondack chairs. God what I wouldn't give to be able to sit in those chairs sipping iced tea for the next fifty years.

"You heard me," Mike said with a bit of cockiness in his tone as he smirked in my direction, "we are going mudding." Of course, I had heard the term countless times before, after all I did live in Georgia, but I've never been one to actually go mudding.

I looked down at what I was wearing and I supposed it would suffice although the flip flops would make walking rather hard in the mud. He said we could get a little dirty not a little muddy. And then I looked over to him and it suddenly all made sense. No wonder he looked like he was getting ready to go to the shop, he knew that we were going to end up getting filthy.

He was decked out in these sexy as sin tattered up old jeans, holes were worn in the knees. You could buy jeans like these nowadays, but these weren't factory made. All kinds of hard work went into those jeans. The shirt he was wearing, if it could even still be called a shirt, was just some old, faded t-shirt that had the sleeves cut off basically from the collar down, so there was very little shirt covering his skin. From this angle, with him sitting in the driver's seat, I could see just the briefest hint of hair smattering over his chest. And dare I say that I could perfectly see his nipples, which made me giddy because they made my mouth water just thinking about biting them. Topped off with an old pair of work boots and his seen better days baseball cap. I think that would be the first thing I did when I got a job, buy him a new baseball cap so he didn't have the wear the old ratty one anymore.

Wait, back the truck up. I think I was officially crazy, me thinking about biting his nipples. But in my defense he was a heaping of sexy. I had told him that we were friends, which why I did that I hadn't even the slightest bit of an explanation. Anxiety I guess, I thought that if I just issued that friend card that things would be better for us, and really they had. I could absolutely without a doubt call him my best friend. We have had so much fun lately, staying up late watching old *Roseanne* reruns, making dinner together, even just sitting on the back patio talking about anything and everything.

But then there was that tiny part of me that absolutely wanted this man. Ok, if we were being honest, a big part of me wanted him. I knew everything he had been through and I could tell that he was happier than he had been in the past, but there was that little inkling telling me that I needed to keep things between us in a friendly territory.

I felt a little nudge at my shoulder and realized I had checked out and it was Mike pushing me.

"Ass, what was that for?"

"If you don't want to go mudding we don't have to. I thought it would be something fun to do." I guess he took my silence as being opposed to this adventure outing.

"Nope, we are already here. Let's do it! I'm not really wearing the right kind of footwear for mud, but I'm not afraid to get dirty."

"You probably won't get as muddy as you think. We will be in a truck the entire time so your feet won't need to touch the ground. If you like going mudding in my truck sometime we can come back and take a ride around on the four-wheelers, but with you just having your boot taken off yesterday, I didn't want to risk you getting injured again."

My heart actually skipped a frigging beat that he was concerned with me getting hurt.

"So we are going to take this truck in the mud?"

He immediately scoffed then started softly caressing the dashboard of his truck. "Don't you listen to her, she didn't mean it." Then he looked at me, "The Beast will *not* be going into the mud. I've put too much time and money in her for her to deliberately get dirty."

Ok, was it only funny to me that he called his truck the Beast and it was also apparently a girl? What was with boys and their toys? I guess I'll never understand.

"Well, *excuse* me," I annunciated every word in a mocking tone. I loved being able to be a smart ass to him anytime I wanted.

But what I didn't anticipate was him leaning over the center console and grabbing my chin as he said sternly but with the hint of smile on his face, "Your smart mouth is going to get you in trouble one of these days."

Oh my God! Cue damp panties. I felt a liquid rush to my core and I wanted to bait him more to see how far he would go. Seriously, Mike shouldn't make promises he didn't intend to keep.

I was thoroughly surprised that by him grabbing my chin it didn't trigger some kind of unwarranted reaction, if anything I wanted more of demanding Mike.

He hopped out of the Beast and came around to open my door and to offer his hand in helping me down. My foot was healed, but still on the weaker side, so I was very thankful for his help.

I followed him up the gravel driveway towards a detached garage which looked like it would hold at least ten cars. Ok, I may have been exaggerating a little, but it came pretty close.

"Whose house is this?" I asked while looking around for a sign of anyone else, but coming up short.

"This is Ray Monroe's house, Brock's dad and owner of Ray's Auto where I help out sometimes. Brock should be in the garage, he and his wife Tessa are going to come out with us."

This was news, and although I'd met Brock I was excited to meet his wife.

He opened the door to the garage and urged me to step in, once I stepped over the threshold I couldn't believe what all I saw. This was truly a country boy's wet dream. I started taking everything in until I looked directly to my right and came almost face to face with an animal, one that probably could have outran me.

I swear I jumped six feet high and directly into the arms of Mike. "Holy shit, what is *that?*" I clung to Mike as he wrapped his arms around me.

He whispered into my ear, "It's ok Sheridan. It's not real."

"Oh, ok." I felt pretty stupid as I started sliding my body down his chest and he immediately did a quick intake of breath.

I heard someone coming up behind Mike chuckling, so I quickly let go the rest of the way from Mike and looked over to see Brock and a beautiful blonde coming our way.

"Now don't let him fool you. That there moose head is most definitely real. My dad killed it on his hunting trip to Alaska last year, he had the taxidermist mount the head for him, and he just hasn't gotten around to bracketing it up higher."

Brock clarified.

I put my hand over my still racing heart, "Well that thing almost gave me a heart attack. That is seriously friggin creepy."

"Tell me about it, if that freaks you out don't go into the house. I seriously don't know how Brock's mom lives with all of the stuffed creepy critters that are in that house. Blake, our almost two year old, thinks they are the funniest things. I'm Tessa, Brock's wife," she came forward with her outstretched hand, introducing herself to me.

"Sheridan, nice to meet you. So are you going mudding with us?"

"You bet your sweet bippy I am. I'm so excited that a girl around here wants to actually go mudding. I've tried to get my best friends Emmalynne and Toby out here forever. Toby is afraid of messing up his manicure and Emmy just flat out refuses, although now with a newborn, she has an excuse."

She turned around to walk away and I looked at Mike with a questioning look on my face and mouthed, "Sweet bippy?"

Mike chuckled, "Just go with it. Tessa is…different. She'll say some weird things, just a warning. Come on."

I followed him throughout the garage, we passed several different ATVs and dune buggies, even a few dirt bikes were in the mix. There were several locked gun cabinets lined against the back wall and Craftsman tool chests filled with I'm sure every tool imaginable.

This truly was a man's haven. The ultimate outdoor store blew up inside of this garage.

Mike realized that I was still lingering about and cleared his throat to get my attention. Meeting his eyes, he said, "Over here."

He stopped in front of a truck that had really seen better days, that was the wrong term. This poor truck should've been put to rest decades ago, it was decrepit.

"Will this truck break down on us?" It was a legitimate question.

"No, it won't break down," he said in a mocking tone while making a funny expression with his mouth. He slapped a hand on the hood of the truck and actual dirt billowed up from where his hand met the metal. *That* did nothing to reassure me in the slightest.

I looked at the truck even more as I walked around it, I wanted to do a thorough inspection even though I had no clue what in the world I was doing. On the back tailgate, I had to giggle because apparently it used to be a Dodge and now it just was a Dog indicated by the vehicle insignia letters on the back. The color was now a mixture of primer and rust, but I did have to say it had the biggest tires I had ever seen on any type of vehicle. That had to account for something. It reminded me of a Bigfoot truck, just not as nice anymore.

He opened the door for me, like a true gentleman, and waved a hand indicating it was now time to get in, "Your chariot awaits." He put his hands on my hips and hoisted me up into the truck. My, oh my, did I love those little subtle touches from him, his hands could linger for the briefest of time but it would still send electricity soaring throughout my body.

I needed a cool breeze, it was officially getting hot in here.

I situated my butt on the seat, which wasn't in the greatest condition either, but then again why would you take a nice looking vehicle out in the mud and woods to get damaged? You'd be pretty messed up in the head to do that.

The floorboards were ripped free of the carpeting and there was dried mud everywhere.

I looked out the front windshield and something sticking out from the hood piqued my attention. Mike climbed into the truck and saw my quizzical expression.

"What are you looking at?" He looked out of the

windshield to try to get a glimpse of what was befuddling me.

I raised my finger and pointed at the odd looking contraption and said, "Is that a snorkel?"

He tipped his head back and really belted out a laugh, one that came from deep inside your belly. It put a smile on my face to know that I could get such a reaction out of him. I definitely loved this side of him and would choose it over rude, broody Mike any day.

"Sweet-uh-Sheridan, that is a snorkel," he caught himself before the word was entirely out of his mouth. I was torn whether I was happy or sad about that. "This entire truck had to be modified for mud boggin'. Much of the same modifications that I did for the Beast I did for this one as well, such as the suspension lift, which raises the entire truck giving you enough clearance to go over higher terrain. But this truck also has mud tires and the snorkel. The snorkel is used so the exhaust fumes expel from it instead of underneath the truck. It helps so the transmission doesn't get flooded. This truck is amazing at off road excursions and driving in the mud."

And I was lost. "Ok, I didn't really understand half of that, but then again I don't speak man. So I'll just take your word for everything."

I was getting excited I began searching for my seatbelt and clicked it in place. I placed my feet on the dashboard getting all giddy. I looked over at Mike and he had a humorous expression and I said, "I'm ready! Do I need a helmet or anything?"

He chuckled again, but not as deep, "You are too damn cute," which instantly made me feel the heat creep up into my cheeks. "But no, you don't need a helmet. I'll be taking things pretty easy today since this is your first time."

"Hey!" Tessa yelled from outside of the truck. I turned to see her decked out in a pair of coveralls with a short sleeved shirt on underneath them. I was kind of glad to be in the confines of an automobile, it's too hot to be wearing pants outside. She had a helmet tucked underneath her arm and said, "You ready to get 'er done?"

I gave her a thumbs up the same time that she placed the helmet over her head and Mike fired up the Dog.

Pulling back into the drive leading up to the garage, Mike put the mud caked truck into park. He quickly came over and helped me down before he went to retrieve a hose so he could spray off some of the big clumps of mud from the truck.

Even being out of the truck and onto solid ground I still felt as if I were bouncing around in the cab as Mike traveled over the rough terrain and through the mud pits.

I had to literally hold my breasts down during the impact of the bumps and holes that he hit, and he seemed to hit every single last one of them. I think in a demented way he liked seeing me in pain. Luckily my boobs weren't just a bit bigger or I'd run the risk of blacking an eye. Next time, if there would be a next time because besides the casualty of my boobs I really had enjoyed myself, I would definitely be either taping these puppies down or wearing a regular bra plus a sports bra over top.

Brock and Tessa were on their way back, they had a bet going on who could win out of the two of them racing back here. And the loser had to clean off both of the four-wheelers before they were put up in the garage for the night.

You could hear the rumble of the ATV engines as they roared up next to the filthy truck.

Tessa made it just seconds before Brock and she put it into park and started revving the engine as she pulled off her helmet and yelled at Brock, "Ha! Put that in your pipe and smoke it!"

Mike and I looked to each other and just smiled, she was pretty quirky, but she was hard not to like.

"How about we go in for some iced tea while you men finish cleaning the mud off of everything?"

Tessa was speaking to me, but I automatically looked to Mike to see him nodding encouraging me to go on.

I followed Tessa in through the backdoor which was the laundry room that led straight into the kitchen. The kitchen was picturesque but extremely outdated. I would explain it as a country kitchen that opened to the dining room but was separated by a bar.

Tessa went to the white fridge and pulled out a glass pitcher filled with tea and filled four glasses near the rim that she had retrieved from the cupboard.

"You're good for him." She meagerly stated.

"Oh, we aren't together," I felt the need to correct her. I didn't want her to think that we were something that we weren't.

"Sure you aren't. And I'm not Tessa Monroe, I'm Marilyn. Just keep telling yourself that."

Just then a little boy came toddling into the kitchen from the other room, he caught a glimpse of Tessa and with a big toothy grin said, "Momma!" while he had his arms outstretched towards her. She immediately scooped him up and gave him a big kiss on his head.

Seeing the affection between mother and child made me feel devastated.

I had my hand on my chest, the pounding of my racing heart beat against it, and I could feel my breath begin to accelerate; I knew I was close to having a panic attack. I had to brace myself against the bar as I could feel my legs weakening. They had been pretty scarce as of late, but sometimes certain things triggered them. I didn't want to appear rude, but I really needed to get out of here.

"Sheridan this is my son, Blake."

She had yet to look at me, so I thought I could mask my unease and sneak on out of here.

"Hi, Blake," I said but my voice cracked. I was busted.

Tessa looked up at me and instantly had the look of concern on her face, "Sheridan are you alright?"

I tried to wave it off as best as I could, but still had tremors in my voice, "I'll be fine, just not feeling very well."

I pushed myself off the counter and prayed to God that I could make my way back outside at least to where I could sit in the truck.

I came upon the truck and Mike and Brock were carrying on laughing until they saw my face. Mike's face fell as he rushed up to me, putting his hands on my forearms to steady me.

"Sheridan are you alright?" He had a worried tremor in his voice. "Take slow deep breaths."

"I'm fine, I just don't feel well."

He looked past me and must've seen Tessa because his eyes hardened.

He escorted me towards The Beast so we could leave.

"I'm sorry guys, Sheridan isn't feeling well. Put my truck back in the garage will ya?"

"Sure," Brock said while waving a hand at us, "feel better soon Sheridan. We had fun today, we'll have to do it again!"

Mike hoisted me up into the truck and helped me clasp my seatbelt. I leaned against the glass window and tried to take deep breaths.

Who knew that seeing a little boy would send me into such a tailspin?

HAPTER 13

Mike

During the ride home, Sheridan really didn't make a peep. I thought things were going well then she came out looking like she was terrorized.

"Tessa didn't say anything to you, did she?" Tessa was normally an easy person to get along with and I really couldn't imagine her saying anything hurtful towards Sheridan unless she was provoked. And Sheridan wasn't the one to do that.

"No, it was nothing like that." And that was all she had to say the remainder of the ride home.

I had to turn on the radio to cut through the deafening silence.

Low and behold the radio knew exactly what song we needed right now. "I Want You To Want Me" by Cheap Trick was currently playing on the classic rock station. I definitely wanted her to want me and I think in her own way she did. Perhaps she thought that we were such good friends that taking it further would hurt things, just as I did, but I was almost past the point of worrying about it. I needed her more. We were amazing together as friends, I honestly thought we would be phenomenal as lovers.

I couldn't tell you exactly what started playing next, because it did absolutely nothing to drown out the onslaught of my thoughts.

We had an amazing day, I didn't think I had ever heard Sheridan giggle and laugh so much. I could feel my heart expanding at every little smile she gave me. I thought that if things kept up the way that they were I could see my heart being almost fully restored. Of course, there would always be that broken piece that would never quite fit back with the rest of it. But Sheridan made me happy, she made my heart happy.

I really needed to get to working on her car, especially since she was so excited to find a job. I couldn't keep her here forever, but it sure as hell wouldn't be for my lack of trying.

My accidentally almost calling her sweetheart, she looked both relieved and perturbed. My attraction to her was growing not waning in the least bit, I was going to end up acting on my attractions and it would be sooner rather than later. I just hope it didn't ruin things when my resolve would eventually fade. I had to have her, make her mine.

When I saw Tessa come out with Blake perched upon her hip, I instantly wanted to leave. Maybe Sheridan felt awkward around children too.

"Sheridan?" I waited a beat to see if she would turn her head and look at me and I was rewarded with her eyes, but it was almost a punch to the gut at the miserable look on her face.

"Sheridan, do you want children?" I wanted to know if this would be a deal breaker for us. I didn't think I could submit myself to that ever again and well, if she did, then I could easily tell that this attraction between us wasn't going to go any further than that.

Her eyes darkened and she looked almost ferocious, as she spoke up saying more than just a few words the entire time we've been on the road. "Remember when I said that I escaped for eleven months a little over three years ago?" I nodded following along in her explanation. "Well, I never knew if Pate would come find me, so I took measures to where I couldn't have any more children, *Mike.*"

The way she put the emphasis on my name with such finality, I knew that she was finished conversing, so I just let her stew in her own thoughts the rest of the way home.

Once I pulled onto my concrete covered driveway, she didn't wait for me to put my truck into park, she had already thrown open the passenger side door, slammed it shut, and was halfway to the front door before I was even able to get out of the truck. I raced up so I could open the door for her only for her to storm past me and then halt in her tracks. She whirled around to face me, still not even a little sign of her mood changing, "I'm going to go call my mom, and I'd really like to be left alone." And that was the last I saw of her that night.

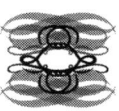

Waking up at the first sight of the sun wasn't the way I wanted this day to start, but with my constant restless tossing and turning, I didn't see any additional sleep in sight. So I threw my sheet off of my legs and sat up in bed using the palms of my hands to wipe away any remaining sleep from my eyes.

I didn't know how the day would go since Sheridan disappeared to her room once we got home from mudding yesterday. The only peep I heard coming out of her room last night was the sound of her keyboard. She kept playing different lullabies, and it reminded me so much of the nursery rhymes that Hannah would enjoy.

Sheridan may not show it or talk about it much, but losing her baby affected her more than she thought. At least I got to spend three wonderful years with my princess, she wasn't even able to hold her precious miracle. What a double-edged sword, I'm thankful that I had time with my Hannah but then again, maybe it hurt more for me because I had time with Hannah. Grief is grief I supposed.

Sadie perked her head up at the end of the bed and started wagging her tail because my attention was focused on her. She hadn't been receiving as much attention from me lately because I've been focusing mine on Sheridan, but she had really taken to Sheridan. Even to the point of whining at her door last night because Sheridan walked past her without giving her any lovin'.

I decided that I was going to take Sadie on a walk first thing before I accomplished anything else for the day, which would include trying to get Sheridan out of her funk.

I slipped on a pair of jersey basketball shorts, an old gray t-shirt, and then slipped my old baseball cap over my unmanaged hair and went out into the hall where I was promptly greeted by Sheridan. She immediately smiled brightly and greeted me with, "Good morning!" Wow, talk about a complete one-eighty from yesterday, someone had a sunny disposition this morning. I just wish I was up to her level of cheery and alertness.

She looked down and bent over grabbing Sadie's head in both of her hands and leaned over and gave her a big kiss atop of her head. "Good morning, Sadie Belle! Who is a good girl?" She cooed as she rubbed behind her ears. I have never in my life been jealous of an animal, especially my dog, but in that moment I wanted to be the one getting kissed on my head. It wouldn't have been my ideal location, but any kiss from Sheridan couldn't have been bad. It sucked that I was actually green with envy because of Sadie getting the attention, wow I had personally stooped to a new low.

"Ahem," I cleared my throat and announced that I was taking Sadie for a walk, so I would be the good guy again, the favorite in Sadie's eyes. "After we get back would you like to go to The Diner for breakfast? I've never taken you there and it has an amazing atmosphere and equally amazing grease, I mean food."

My intentional slip of the tongue earned me a smile from Sheridan which made my heart beat double time. I was officially in trouble, I supposed I had been since the first time I caught sight of her sitting in her wrecked car, but I never fully realized the extent until now.

I was in *big* trouble.

"Sure, greasy food sounds amazing right now. Um," she looked down at her hands which were tangled together as she fidgeted with them, "I wanted to apologize for last night. I didn't act the way that I should have. It just brought back a lot of harbored feelings last night seeing Tessa and her son together, happy."

I quickly brought up my hand halting her apology, "Absolutely no worries, I felt quite awkward myself whenever she came outside with him. No matter how cute Blake is, and I know that he isn't Hannah, I just can't bring myself to be around him. It hurts too much and makes me remember things that I try to bury."

She moved closer to me placing her hand on my shoulder, her illuminating eyes focused on mine, "Mike you shouldn't try to bury your memories. Those are the good things that remain between you and Hannah. I know you aren't trying to forget her, but you shouldn't bury her memory as well. Embrace the time that you two shared together. Try talking about different things from when she was a child, it may help. And remember, I'll always be here for you."

I stood there long after Sheridan went into the bathroom just thinking about what she had said to me. Since that day, I had talked to a few people about how amazing and precious Hannah was, but I never really went into detail about what made her so special. Perhaps if I started speaking about different instances my heart wouldn't hurt as much whenever I thought of her. I didn't have to think of her as being gone all the time, I could think of the fond memories we shared.

I felt as if my steps were getting lighter as I walked down the hallway to retrieve Sadie's leash. She was excited to go and was currently showing me how excited as she chased her tail around the living room. Silly dog.

Arriving in front of The Diner, I could tell that Sheridan was excited as her eyes lit up at the appearance of the building. It made me mentally chide myself for not bringing her here sooner.

Think retro 50s diner and you had The Diner. It was truly authentic retro complete with the old-fashioned aluminum siding. It sat a little off of the beaten path but was literally right around the corner from Ray's Auto.

When first walking inside Sheridan stopped right in front of an aqua gas pump gumball machine. She turned around, a beaming smile on her face, "I love this place! I had no idea it even existed."

She began wandering aimlessly around taking in all of the tin signs that hung on the walls even tracing her fingertips along the outside semi-circle frame of the old vintage jukebox. It has been completely restored, but was in full working condition, belting out the 50s classics that I grew up listening to with my dad.

"Can we sit anywhere?" Sheridan asked eyeing the seating arrangements.

I nodded my head and I thought that she would sit at the bar on one of the red leather topped barstools but I was completely surprised when she took a seat in one of the red and black leather covered booth bench seats.

I slid myself in opposite her and she already had her laminated menu out perusing through the breakfast dining choices.

"So what's good here?" she asked, not even taking her eyes off of the menu.

"Everything is phenomenal. I haven't ever had anything here that I didn't like. The ambiance is what sets the entire restaurant. Archie and Wanda have done an amazing job at keeping this place up and going."

She made a little giggle noise from the back of her throat and arched a brow at me.

"What?" I asked.

"Their names are Archie and Wanda? That sounds just like someone who would own a diner like this, totally cute."

"Yeah, you won't think that it's cute after having being married to him for over thirty years," Wanda came up to the booth and said.

A faint blush swept through Sheridan's cheeks at the thought of being caught talking about Archie and Wanda, but they were seriously the nicest couple. Bickered relentlessly back and forth between each other, but it was done out of nothing but love for the other person.

Wanda wore her normal uniform of a button down white oxford shirt and a black skirt, she now claims that she was too old to wear the other waitress uniform. But, on the other hand, Sheridan would be a complete knockout in it. All she would need to do was wear her crimson lipstick, the one I love so much, and have her hair pulled up in a retro way and she would be a fucking bombshell.

I could feel the occupying free space in my jeans quickly fill up due to my imaginative thoughts of Sheridan, but God she would look edible.

I needed to quickly think of something else, food. Food

was always a good distraction. I began looking at my own menu trying to decide what I wanted to eat.

After chatting with Wanda for just a few minutes, she took our orders as The Diner began filling up.

Wanda worked every single day and only had a handful of people to work with her. There was no question that she needed more help.

I was getting ready to make small talk when Charlie Hennings came up to the table. I had to quickly do a double take because he was wearing a Sheriff's uniform. I hadn't seen him since the altercation that occurred and Maggie's kidnapping.

I knew Sheriff Mitchell would be resigning and moving out of state, but I had no idea that Charlie was the replacement. I wondered why Brock hadn't told me.

"Hey guys," he said looking at each of us. Sheridan had a brief wondering look in her eye, until she nonchalantly nodded her head, she must have just remembered who he was.

"Hey, Charlie, you remember Sheridan," I waved my hand in her direction.

"Yeah, I was with Maggie when you had your accident." He didn't look very happy about mentioning Maggie's name. I'm guessing that things didn't work out between the two of them, but it wasn't like I could blame Maggie. Charlie directly lied to her about who he was and what his job pertained to.

"I remember, how are you?" Sheridan replied politely. "Although, I don't recall you being the Sheriff."

"This actually didn't happen until a few weeks ago, and it was official this morning. Well, I don't want to interrupt you two, I was just getting breakfast to go."

We said our mutual goodbyes and Sheridan was still casually looking around, just taking in the scenery.

I wondered if she knew how beautiful she was. When and if the opportunity arose, I would tell her every chance that I could.

I had heard Archie ring the bell a few times now, indicating that an order was ready. But Wanda was still with customers. Sheridan noticed the same thing as well and the counter which held the ready to be served food was quickly filling up.

Sheridan looked one last time back at Wanda, "I'll be right back." She said to me as she rose up from the booth and walked over right to the serving counter. She exchanged a few words with Archie, who pointed to a table and then handed her two plates.

I really couldn't believe that Sheridan was helping Wanda out. If it were Erin, she would've been here bitching because we had to wait on our food. This just proved that they were two entirely different people. And what I felt for Erin wasn't even half as strong as I felt for Sheridan and I wasn't even full blown in love with her yet.

Love was a funny thing, here I never thought I would love another living thing, but Sheridan finagled her way into my life and into my heart.

She looked over to me and smiled brightly before placing the dishes down in front of their respective owners.

After serving a few more plates, she stood in front of our table, sitting down her plate and then making a grand gesture by placing mine in front of me, "Your order, kind sir," she said in a silly manor and immediately giggled afterwards.

"Why thank you, madam," I had to keep up the charade. "I really can't believe you just helped out, you are a really good person Sheridan."

She faintly smiled and sheepishly shrugged her shoulders before grabbing her fork and digging into her stuffed French toast.

She had no idea what it was like to be complimented, and wasn't that a shame because she deserved so many compliments.

Bringing the first bite to her mouth, I saw the tines of her fork disappear and I swear her eyes rolled back in her head as she moaned. "Oh my God," she said while she still had a mouth full of food, but she quickly covered her mouth with her hand. "I'm so sorry, but it is *so* damn good."

Each and every single bite she savored over and it was making it extremely hot in The Diner. I had to continuously pull my shirt off of my chest, to get a little air in order to breathe. These little sounds she was making each and every time her fork entered her mouth was ultimately going to be the death of me.

Wanda came up to the end of our booth and stuck her hip out and perched her hand that was holding her notepad upon it. She directed a pointed stare at Sheridan and shoved her pencil towards her face. Just when I thought Wanda was going to give her a serious tongue lashing, she surprised the hell out of me, "Now what I can't understand is why someone would help serve dishes without any type of incentive. You don't find that type of kindness much nowadays anymore."

I spoke up before Sheridan could reply, "Well, Sheridan is a truly extraordinary person."

Sheridan looked down at her plate as a pink hue tinged her cheeks.

I had to mentally pat myself on the back for being able to compliment her again. I was almost taken aback at the reaction she had to them. It just went to show that you should never judge a book by its cover, as I had done with Sheridan in the beginning.

She looked so extremely put together on the outside and you would almost assume she would come across as uppity, and even though she could be a major smartass, she was such a genuine person. I couldn't believe that Pate dragged her and her confidence down with his actions and words. I wanted to see that rosiness in her cheeks all the time, I needed to step up my game.

"You were busy, I didn't want things to get backed up for you guys." She spoke softly and shrugged a slumped shoulder while moving her fork across her half eaten French toast.

Wanda looked at me and winked while I cracked a half smile.

"Well, how would you like to actually do that for pay?"

Sheridan straightened her posture and instantly perked up, "You mean like work here?"

Wanda looked at me once again but this time with a stunned expression and then pointed her pencil back at Sheridan, "Is this cat for real?" She turned back to Sheridan, "Honey this job isn't that glamorous. It's hard work, you get shitty people and bust your ass for even shittier pay."

"Well, when you put it that way, sure!" I could tell Sheridan was ecstatic by the twinkle in her eyes.

"Be here tomorrow morning at nine am sharp, don't be late," she gave her a hard stare before turning around to walk away from us.

I leaned forward with my elbows resting on the table and said in a hushed tone, "Don't let the old bitty fool ya, she loves working here and all of her customers."

"Yeah, you just keep on telling yourself that!" Wanda yelled over her shoulder in her raspy voice.

I laughed and then brought my attention back to Sheridan who looked as if she were about to burst at the seams with excitement.

"Go ahead, get it out."

She let out a little high pitched shrill as she stomped her feet on the floor and shook her hands out in front of her. It made me happy to see her so excited about something.

"So, now that you officially have a job in Brown County do you think you will make it a permanent residence?"

She stopped her little happy dance and locked eyes on mine. Her eyes seemed to flare as she tried to regain her normal breathing. "Well, let's see here, I have a car that will *hopefully* be in functioning order soon," I liked how she had to sneak in a little dig at me, but she was right, I needed to get it in top shape for her to drive, "I now have a job in this quaint little retro joint, I have new people to call friends to surround my life with, I would have to say that I could definitely see Brown County becoming home. Now all I need to do is find someplace to live and get a few other important things and everything would be perfect."

I didn't know what other important things she was referring to, but I didn't like her thinking that she had to move out and find a residence of her own.

"You know Sheridan, my spare bedroom is yours for however long you want it. I want to make sure that you are up on your feet and stable before you trouble yourself with looking for a house."

"Why, Mike I would almost believe that you liked having me around."

I guess it was my turn to get a sheepish expression on my face, but I quickly recovered, "Well you know, I guess you're alright to have around and besides Sadie would miss you."

I settled our bill and she shoulder checked me on the way out to my truck, "Alright, you don't have to admit it but I would miss being around you too."

It had been a few weeks since Sheridan started working at The Diner and her presence at home had been very scarce. She was working all the time, picking up extra shifts and sometimes doubles. I would offer her a ride whenever I could, but she would often turn me down wanting to walk. It just showed the initiative she had and the ability to persevere. It was safe to say that I was turning into a girl with feelings, because I missed the hell out of her. I missed our daily smart ass banter and Sadie missed her lounge buddy.

It's amazing how quickly someone could settle into a normal routine and although I loved that Sheridan had a job, especially one that she was happy at, I hated that our 'routine' had been upturned.

The very first day of working at The Diner she came home in such a happy mood and was carrying a large white sack. That next morning she came out of the bathroom in her new work uniform, which was what had been in the sack. I had to almost quite literally catch my jaw before it fell on the floor.

Holy fucking pin-up model, she was smokin'.

I couldn't tell you exactly what type of expression she saw on my face, but it must not have what she was aiming for.

"Does it not look ok?"

I was seriously struck dumb by her beauty.

I started at her feet, because looking up any further for a continuous amount of time would result in a lower piece of my anatomy severely inflating, and I couldn't have that with the current position I was in.

She had just plain black ballet flats on her feet, but what I wouldn't have given to see her in a pair of red peep toe pumps. Shit, starting with her feet was supposed to help me calm down not get me even more riled up.

Traveling up her long, shapely legs, I found the hem of her Fifties style retro dress. This particular dress was black with little red cherries all over it. She had her little white apron wrapped around her waist and tied in the front in a big red bow. The top of the dress was what really took the cake, it was almost in a heart shape. The rounded portion of the heart covering the swell of her breasts. But that little dip in the middle that separated the two halves revealed a pretty nice portion of her cleavage.

"Ahem," Sheridan cleared her throat, and I realized that I was still staring at her breasts and hadn't answered her question. "My eyes are up here you know." I quickly flicked my eyes up to her face and then saw that she had taken the stance of a pissed off woman; hip protruding out and a hand perched on it, the only thing that would complete this look would be her toe tapping on the floor.

"Sheridan, you look...wow! You look absolutely beautiful, I'm just really glad that Wanda doesn't wear the same uniform, I don't really know who could pull it off better."

Hands down it was Sheridan.

Her face broke out in a smile, which made her outlined crimson lips look amazing against the whiteness of her teeth. She even stayed true to the theme of the diner with her hair, it was done up in some retro like twist. God if she would just start strutting and sashaying around singing "Happy Birthday, Mr. President," in a sexy tone, I would seriously die a happy man, it would be with an extremely horrendous case of blue balls, but I would be happy nonetheless.

Sadie whining at the door broke me out of my Sheridan induced trance, she must have been home from work. I straightened myself up on the couch, it was my day off and I actually for once took the day off. I did absolutely nothing but piddle around the house and watch crap TV but it was nice to be able to just relax for once instead of trying to run myself in a million different directions.

The storm door opened and I heard Sheridan's special high pitched voice, reserved especially for Sadie, "Hi there Sadie Belle, have you been a good girl today?" Sadie whimpered a few more times and it was almost as if she was trying to answer her question.

I heard the clicking of her shoes on my hardwood floor before I saw her appear in the doorway to the living room. She looked surprised to see me home, especially being on the couch,

"Oh, hey Mike. I didn't know you'd be home." She came walking around the back of the couch and around the other side to sit opposite me, "And watching *Roseanne* too? Do you have a fever, are you feeling alright?" She leaned over to place the back of her hand on my forehead. I knew she was just joking with me but it felt nice being cared for.

Her being in the position she was in gave me the perfect view of her cleavage and I had to quickly recover before I started salivating over her luscious breasts.

I scratched my arm to give my hands something to do, which was becoming more and more common these days, if my hands were free they would itch to touch Sheridan, to hold her. "What can I say, there wasn't anything else on. It was either this or *Real Housewives* of some rich community. And I really didn't feel like listening to catty bitches fight, so *Roseanne* won."

"Well, I'm glad you're here." My ears perked up a little more. "I received my first paycheck at The Diner today so I wanted to get you a little something to thank you for everything you've done. It's nothing much, but I hope you like it."

She handed over a small bag and I hurriedly tried to rustle it open. I wasn't used to receiving gifts, this was unchartered territory for me, but I was happy that Sheridan thought of me.

I took the item out of the bag and just looked at it blankly. My heart lurched into my throat and I honestly didn't know what to say.

The item in the bag was a navy blue St. Louis Cardinals baseball cap. Almost identical to the tattered one that I always wore except it didn't have the giant red cardinal on the side like my current one had.

She pointed to the hat, "I saw it and instantly thought of you. Now you can replace the dingy one that you always wear." I still couldn't speak and she began to get extremely fidgety at my lack of a response. "Is it not ok? I mean you must like the Cardinals since you wear it all the time, but one thing I had never really took into consideration is that you don't have a single bit of other Cardinals memorabilia in your house. Diehard fans normally have their space decked out in it."

I just continued staring at the new hat that Sheridan gave me, but finally found my voice and it came out harsher than I had intended it to, "That's because I'm not a diehard fan actually, I really hate the Cardinals."

I rose from the couch the new hat clutched in one hand and the sack it came in clutched in the other. I began walking towards my room, I needed to be alone at the present time.

"Then why do you wear it, especially to the point of it almost falling apart?"

I stopped my descent and turned back towards the couch to see Sheridan twisted in her seat, "I received this hat on my birthday from Hannah a few weeks before she died. She liked the red cardinal on the side of and thought it would look good on me."

I turned back around to finish my way to my room and I heard Sheridan take a sharp intake of breath. I knew it wasn't her fault, she didn't know, but I really couldn't bear to console her at the moment and assure her that everything was ok. I promptly shut my door and just laid outstretched on my back in my bed for the rest of the night.

CHAPTER 14

Sheridan

It had been a few days since my gift giving disaster occurred. Things were almost back to normal I supposed. Mike finally had reassured me that I didn't know so it wasn't a big deal, but I knew it had to have brought up some daunting memories for him.

No wonder he wore the thing until the stitches were coming out of the seams, his princess had given it to him. When his explanation came out of his mouth I instantly felt sick. Of all the things that I could have given him, it was the one thing that should never be replaced.

It was a busy day at The Diner and I didn't see an end to the mass amounts of customers in sight and of course, it had to be a day that I agreed to work over my normal eight hour shift.

The customers instantly took to me and I tried to make my cheery disposition the first thing they encountered when entering for their meals, this had made for some fantastic tips. But today just wasn't a good day, my feet ached and my hands hurt. I just prayed that I wouldn't drop anything.

My usual customers had already come and gone, Charlie

being one of them. He had been in to grab his breakfast every day that he was on shift, which was normally every day. He always looked so sad and generally needed some cheering up, so I always made sure I wore my biggest smile in hopes that it would rub off on him.

It was weird to think that I had regular customers. I now even have people request to sit in my section when they saw me working. Wanda was more than alright with it because it took some of the workload off of her.

She really almost reminded me of Roseanne except for her fiery red hair. She was almost pushing sixty but acted as if she were thirty. The poor woman was so busty and it caused her to have major back pain because of it. She always acted like she couldn't care less or didn't give a shit, but something in her eyes told me otherwise. She was trying to put up a tough exterior for some reason or another, but I had seen through her antics. I had really grown quite fond of her. You always knew when she was coming because of her huffing and puffing due to being an excessive chain smoker, her poor voice had even turned raspy because of it. She was always taking a break to go light up one of her cigarettes, but I didn't mind because I had a job.

I was bringing plates to their respective tables left and right, no time for resting and I could feel my hands getting weaker, but I chose to ignore it.

The next plate that I grabbed shouldn't have affected my hand, it was only filled with pancakes, but that was how my hands worked. It could be the smallest of things, but when they wanted to give out they just did. No rhyme or reason to it.

I felt the plate slip out of my hand and away from my grasp as it fell to the black and white tiled floor and shattered into dozens of pieces.

I was instantly thrown back into Pate's house and I just knew he was going to get onto me for ruining another one of his plates. I knelt on the floor trying to pick up the remnants of the plate and prayed to God that he would take it easy on me.

I felt a hand on my shoulder and I instantly began pleading and apologizing profusely, hoping that the blow wouldn't be as harsh.

"I'm so, so sorry. I'm cleaning it up as quickly as I can."

"Sheridan," the raspy voice of Wanda brought me back to the present. I blinked away the thought of Pate and realized that I was still in The Diner. My hands were filled with the remains of a mixture of pancakes and broken ceramic.

I felt tears well up in the corners of my eyes and I again apologized, "I'm so sorry, Wanda. My hands are weak sometimes."

"Girl, don't you worry about it. Happens to the best of us," she waved off. I really liked how she tried to downplay the situation trying to make me feel better. I kept my focus on the scraps on the floor, because I didn't want to see every single eye in the restaurant on me and my clumsy hands.

Archie came up behind me and put a hand on my back, "Why don't you take a break, grab yourself a cup of coffee and take a seat at the counter." He winked and started sweeping up the fragments into a dustpan and disposing of them in the back.

I took a deep breath and let it all out. No matter how good my life was now, I could never ever get rid of the gruesome memories of my past.

I did what was suggested and plopped myself down on one of the barstools and placed my head in my hands. I couldn't quit, accepting defeat wasn't an option. Pate wouldn't win.

I had almost everything I needed here. I was getting my life in order and soon it would be complete. I had Mike, but what the hell were we? He was without a doubt my best friend, but I longed for more. Sometimes I would think that I would see little glimpses of hope for the two of us, but I didn't know if the feeling was mutually reciprocated.

I heard a set of bags being sat down beside me and the

relentless chatter of a male and female. I knew that females voice.

I perked up to see Tessa Monroe sitting next to me.

"Sheridan, I was hoping you would be here! I caught wind from Brock that you worked here now." She had just started ignoring the guy who was with her, which I hadn't recalled ever seeing.

But evidently he wasn't one to be ignored. "Ahem," he said stepping in between Tessa and myself and extending his hand in my direction. "Excuse, Tessa sometimes I think she was born in a barn," which earned him a shove in the shoulder and a scoff coming from Tessa. He rolled his eyes in her direction and continued on, "I'm Toby Morgan, and you are absolutely gorgeous."

I instantly felt the color rise in my cheeks at his abrupt forwardness.

"Oh, Toby get a grip." Tessa looked at me, "Don't worry he wasn't hitting on you, he's gay. And besides," she focused her attention to Toby, "even if you weren't, she's with Mike."

"I'm not *with* Mike, I just sleep with him. No, I meant I sleep in his spare bedroom at his house." I just needed to quit before I kept digging my hole even deeper.

"Uh huh. Don't be ashamed of it girl. If I had a big bad secretive man like Mike, I would be telling everyone that I met on the streets. That boy is fine," Toby quipped. My first impression of him was that he seemed like such a diva. I could almost imagine him snapping his fingers and bobbing his head.

"Oh, I almost forgot," Tessa retrieved one of the plastic sacks from the floor and pulled out a cake mix box and plopped it on the counter in front of me. "Look!"

I looked at Toby and then back at Tessa. Was I missing something here?

"Um yeah, it's a cake mix." I started looking the other way, and then at my imaginary watch, I was thinking that it was almost time for me to be getting back to work.

"No, silly. Its cupcake mix! When Emmalynne had her baby, I tried and tried to find cupcake mix so I could make some cupcakes while she was in the hospital. Everyone freaking looked at me like I was stupid because I didn't realize that I needed cake mix. Well boom! Now what! I found cupcake mix!" She shouted as if she were super proud of herself. I didn't know what to think.

"Right! I'm so happy for you," I tried not to let my sarcasm show, but it was a lost cause.

Toby grabbed me by my shoulder and gave me a half hug, "I like you, you need to hang with us sometime. Or better yet, I need to get the band together and put on a show at Emmy Lou's. Say you'll come if I do! It's been so long since The Nation's Capital has performed, I'm sure Mike is itching to play again."

I faintly remembered Mike stating that he played drums for a band, but he never really talked about it much. It sounded like fun to me, seeing Mike beat on a drum kit with his sticks.

There I went with my sexual innuendos. Oh boy.

"Sure! I'd love to come!"

Toby jumped up and down clapping his hands, "Oh, yay! I'll get everything situated. Come along Tessa, let's not keep Sheridan from her work anymore." He said it almost like chop chop. Wow, there were some fun characters around here.

It was finally seven pm and I was *done* for the day. Mike had texted me earlier saying that he would be at the garage working on my car so I thought it would be nice to bring him a plate of meatloaf from The Diner that he loved so much.

I walked out of The Diner and into the cool summer night air. It was dark enough to see the red neon lights illuminating in the night and the sky was clear enough to see every single star. It was breathtaking. I never really had the time to stop and look at the stars, there were an infinite amount and could be seen for miles. I wish life would always be this simple.

The first thing I did was take down the pins that held up my hair, freeing it from the tight confines of the twist that it was styled in. I ran my fingers through it separating my now curly locks.

Taking my time walking the couple minutes to the garage, I wondered what it would really be like if I was with Mike. He had been attentive and caring already, I just think he would end up stepping it up a notch. I really longed to feel his lips pressed against mine, I bet I would even see fireworks. Oh, but all the wishing and hoping in the world couldn't change the ultimate outcome. Mike and I couldn't be together plain and simple, it just wouldn't work out. We both wanted different things in life.

I walked into the brightly lit garage which heavily smelled of grease and hard work. Justin Timberlake's newest single "Not A Bad Thing" was currently playing on the old boom box. I walked past my car, trailing my hand down it as I went to search for Mike. I didn't have to look too hard, he was currently bent over under the hood of my Monte Carlo with a droplight hanging from the edge of the hood so it would be easier for him to see. He looked so sexy deep in thought with his old hat perched on top of his head.

"Hey," I softly said. I didn't want to startle him, he was so fixated on what he was working on that he hadn't even heard me approach.

He let out a brief sigh and pushed himself up off of the front of my car and started getting things ready so he could close the hood. "Hey Sheridan, I was getting ready to pack up for the night."

"Well, I knew that you said that you'd be working here for a while so I brought you meatloaf from The Diner." I held up the white sack so he could see.

He took the sack containing his to go box and sat it on top of the rolling toolbox that was stationed right next to him. He leaned against it and crossed his arms. "Thanks, what's wrong?"

I had no idea how he could tell anything was wrong, but I couldn't really keep it from him since he knew about my past with Pate. I scooted myself to where I was sitting on the hood of my car, my legs dangling off the edge.

"My hand gave out on me this morning, dropping an entire plate of pancakes all over the floor. I was brought back into the kitchen with Pate hoping that he wouldn't be mad, but knowing that he was fuming inside. Wanda and Archie had to calm me down. I was so embarrassed." I looked down to my hands where I was fiddling with my fingers, "When will it end? When will I finally not feel trapped by him?"

I could feel the tears wanting to well up in my eyes again and I tried so hard to will them away.

I felt Mike's fingertips on my knees as he spread my legs apart so he could step in between them. I could feel my entire body hum at the anticipation of his gentle touches.

He took a hand and placed it underneath my chin and raised my head which caused me to look up into his eyes. The tenderness that was gleaming in his eyes made my heart skip a beat. He took his free hand and gently brushed back the unruly tendrils of hair that wanted to hang in my face.

"Sheridan, you have to give it time. You'll get there, I promise. And I promise that you are undoubtedly safe with me, always. I would lay my life on the line before I ever even thought about letting anything happen to you."

His words held so much conviction and determination that I just wished that things could be different. I wanted to just feel what it would be like to be with him.

He placed his hands under my jaw and just stared into the depths of my eyes. And the next thing I knew, his full lips were pressed tightly to mine.

My eyes were still wide open but seeing his tightly shut I wondered if I should close my eyes and give into my desires just this once? Pretend that things were different?

I suddenly forgot that we weren't able to be together and I just went with the flow of it all. I took the next initiative and swept my tongue along his bottom lip almost begging him for access. One of his hands left the side of my face and ended up gripping my hip and pulling me into him, making me feel the outline of his straining erection. At the same exact time, his tongue entered my awaiting mouth. Our tongues collided together dueling in an intense war. I turned his hat around on his head so it was on backwards and I wouldn't have to worry about my head clashing with it. I grabbed ahold of his shirt tightly wanting nothing more than to be one with this man. This kiss was so intense, I was feeling it all the way down to my toes. He broke free from the kiss and started nipping and kissing his way down my jawline all the way to my collarbone. It was so euphoric and I could just see myself stripping free from my clothing and letting him have his wicked way with me right here on the hood of my car.

But then reality came crashing down on me when I realized that we were in the open bay of Ray's Auto Garage practically mauling one another.

"Mike…" I tried to get his attention, but his focus was on my neck, it was so delicious that I almost hated to put an end to things. "Mike, we can't do this." Kiss. Kiss. Nip. "Mike, stop!"

He released his hold that he had on me so I was able to quickly jump down from my perch from atop of my car.

"What's wrong Sheridan?" His breathing was labored, "I thought you were enjoying it." He looked almost pained at my reaction.

"I did. Believe me, I'm mentally kicking myself now for putting a stop to it, but we just can't. There are just some things that you don't know. Perhaps, if things were different then sure, but they aren't. I'm sorry." I turned to where I could walk out of the shop and I stopped at the edge of the bay door and turned around to see his hands braced on the edge of the rolling tool box and his head hung. We had officially crossed the line into unchartered territory and I didn't know if things could be fixed. "I'll see you at home."

It was now the beginning of August and the blistering heat was showing no signs of cooling down. It was the heart of summer and I was in a rut. A sexually frustrated rut.

If I thought our kiss would've made things awkward between Mike and me; I really couldn't have been more wrong. It didn't turn him off of me, if anything it turned him on more.

It had seemed as if I had opened up Pandora's Box and Mike wasn't backing down from his full on pursuit of me.

He had apparently gotten a taste and wanted more. I wasn't a very strong person as it was and I could almost bet that I would crack sooner than later. But in the end would it be worth it?

Tonight was the night of The Nation's Capital mini concert at Emmy Lou's. Mike had to work at the garage today and then was going to head to the bar with Brock so they could get everything set up and perform a sound check.

Toby and Tessa took me shopping and I picked out an amazing outfit to wear tonight. Toby was upset that he wasn't able to stick around and apply my makeup, apparently he dubbed himself the official makeup artist of Brown County. He was freaking adorable.

So I was getting ready on my own and Tessa was going to swing by on her way to Emmy Lou's and pick me up.

I was freshly showered and pulled on my new ultra skinny jean capris. Seriously these things made my ass look fabulous and they looked like they were painted on, they were so snug. I was so excited to wear my silver beaded V-neck silk tank top that I found on sale. Such an amazing score for such a beautiful top. It was a racer back tank which meant the straps of my bra would've looked extremely tacky, so I had to go strapless. But once I slid the silkiness of my top over my head and let it fall into place on my body, I knew that I would've paid wholesale price for it.

I paired the outfit with turquoise sequined sandals and matching turquoise drop earrings and bracelet. I had mastered the art of French braiding my hair at a young age since I have always had long hair, so I tweaked it a little so it wrapped around my head so it was gathered up off of my neck.

I applied minimal eye shadow but made sure I went heavy on the mascara. And the last thing to perfect the outfit was my fire engine red lipstick. I had never been able to own red lipstick and it was one thing that I had longed for, so on my way out of town when I escaped Pate that was one of the first things that I stopped to purchase. With the color of my skin and the dark black of my hair, I think it paired together nicely.

And I was done.

I looked in the mirror to appraise my look. The outfit was a little more than casual but didn't scream over the top, it was perfection.

No sooner did I gather everything in my turquoise clutch the doorbell rang indicating that Tessa had arrived.

I walked past Sadie Belle and rubbed her head, "You be good and guard the house while we are gone."

I opened the front door and stepped outside closing and locking up behind me.

I turned around to see Tessa staring deadpan at me. I scoffed and said, "What?" as I dropped my keys into my clutch.

"Nothing, you just looking fucking hot!"

I gave her a weird look and shook my head, "Whatever, let's go." And I started making my way towards Tessa's car.

"No, I'm serious. I think I just got my first lady boner.

You are on fi-ya!"

I stopped dead in my tracks and whipped my head around to face Tessa, "Back the truck up! Did you just say that you got a lady boner? What the fuck is a lady boner?"

"Oh, never mind. Come on already," she waved off the complete conversation as if we were discussing the weather and walked on past me to her car. Yikes, I knew Mike said that she said some pretty wonky things, but that was borderline absurd.

When we arrived at Emmy Lou's, I didn't really know what to expect as I had never really been into a bar. Not that Pate would've let me, but I also never really had the desire to.

I followed Tessa in through the sea of people, trying to get a glimpse of everything as I moved. I didn't think so many people would be here, but it was beyond crowded.

She walked straight up to the bar which was located in the back part of the building, wedging herself in between two people, and slammed her hand down on the counter. "Grady!" she yelled trying to get his attention. A guy who I assumed was Grady approached her from behind the counter, he was wearing a black button down shirt with the sleeves rolled up to his elbows. I had seen him in The Diner a few times before, but I never knew who he was.

He seemed less than thrilled to be walking towards Tessa, "What can I get ya Tess?"

"I would like hmm," she put her finger to her chin and started lightly tapping. I think it was just to irritate Grady, and from the way he narrowed his eyes towards her I would have to say that it was indeed working.

"Come on Tessa, we are slammed tonight, Uncle Mac agreed to work for you but ultimately you are here, I could put you to work."

"Ok, ok. Sheesh don't get your panties all in a bunch. I'll have a bottle of Bud. Sheridan this is Grady, he is my best friend Emmalynne's fiancé. Grady this is Sheridan, she works at The

Diner," she cupped her hand to her face and leaned forward a bit and began whispering something to Grady. Unfortunately for her it was still loud enough for me to hear. "She's with Mike."

His eyes widened as he stood up to his full height, "Nice to meet you Sheridan, I believe I've seen you at The Diner a few times."

"Nice to meet you as well, and again for the record I'm not *with* Mike." There was a tremor in my voice and if I were Grady I wouldn't believe the conviction of my words. "I'll just have a Diet Coke, please."

"No alcohol? What the?" Tessa seemed flabbergasted by the fact that I didn't want a drink. I could totally see her telling me that it was "Un-American."

"I don't drink," I turned to glance back at Grady. "Just a Diet Coke, please."

"You got it," he gave me a wink before he turned to get mine and Tessa's drinks.

I perched my elbow on the edge of the countertop and looked around at the space. There were tables lined on the side of the walls so there would be plenty of room to stand around and dance in the middle. The stage was located in the very front and it looked pretty generic with a black curtain running across to shield the crowd from what was happening on stage at the present time.

Grady came back with Tessa's bottle of beer and my Diet Coke in a glass mason jar. I took it from his hand, "Thank you. Um, you wouldn't perhaps have a piano backstage would you?"

He placed a hand on his hip and it looked like he was deep in thought, "You know what, there is an old piano back there but who knows how long it's sat there unused. I'm sure it would need to be tuned."

My lips curved into a bright smile, the thought of being able to play on an actual piano again. My keyboard was amazing and towards the top of the line but it didn't even compare to the eighty-eight keys of an actual piano.

"Would it be alright if I took a look at it sometime?"

"That would be fine by me, you play?" Grady responded as he grabbed the white towel out of his back pocket and began wiping off the condensation from the bar countertop.

"Something like that." I didn't really have it in me to explain my situation to him or to anyone else at the time. Mike knew, and for now that was enough.

The curtains on the stage swept back, the house lights turned down, and a spotlight appeared on Toby.

Tessa yanked at my arm, "Come on, let's move a little closer."

We winded our way through the bar bypassing numerous people she knew as she hooped and hollered at each and every one of them. Finding a free spot directly in the center just being a few feet from the bottom of the stage, I had the perfect view of all of the members.

It was slightly comical seeing Charlie out of his Sheriff's uniform and decked out in a pair of jeans and a t-shirt. Brock was standing just across from him with his guitar slung over his shoulder as well. Toby being the front man was standing, well in the front. Tonight he was donning some black skinny jeans which appeared to be tighter than mine, I really felt sorry for his boys as I had absolutely no idea how they were breathing. And a black fitted tee with a yellow leather bomber jacket with the sleeves pushed up to his elbows. I would ask him how he was keeping from sweating, but I could just imagine him saying, "It's all in the name of fashion, doll."

My gaze then traveled to the man sitting behind the drum kit. The man who seemed to occupy my thoughts at all times of the day. Mike was wearing a pair of cargo khaki shorts and a button down plaid shirt that was rolled up exposing those amazing forearms. He actually wasn't wearing his hat which surprised me because I hadn't ever really seen him out of it. Of course, he didn't wear it when he was working as a paramedic but by the time he came home, his hat was back in its rightful place atop of his head. His dark hair had a messy look going on and it would've been about the exact length which would have made it perfect for me to run my fingers through.

And he was currently staring at me.

Our eyes connected and it was as if the rest of the world diminished and we were the only two people left. I know you hear about that in movies and romance novels, but it was true. I couldn't see the massive amounts of people circled around me, including Tessa who was dancing around like a mad woman.

I had no idea that Toby was even speaking until Tessa shoved me with her shoulder and it released me from my daydream session with Mike.

"Not with Mike my ass. Y'all were practically eye fucking each other. You can keep denying it, but that boy has got it bad for you."

I looked back towards Mike to see that his eyes were still trained on me. Then they started playing their first song.

By the time their last song rolled around Tessa and I had been dancing to their music, they were absolutely fantastic and Toby had a voice that would make the actual singers of the covers cry from embarrassment. Oh and Mike hadn't taken his eyes off of me, not one single time.

They began their last song for the night and Tessa instantly perked up looking behind her for someone in the bar. "Oh, Emmalynne will be so pissed that she isn't here. They are covering her favorite bands newest single "Sleeping With A Friend" by Neon Trees."

The last swallow of my Diet Coke traveled down the wrong tube and I instantly started choking. Tessa lightly pounded on my back until I could catch my breath. What were the odds that they were playing a song about sleeping with a friend?

Mike's gaze had zeroed in even more on me if that was even at all possible.

Toby was traveling around the stage doing little twists and turns as he sang.

It was a different tune for them, but the song was catchy as hell. I found myself singing along to the chorus even though I had never heard of the song or the band before now.

The song actually described Mike and me perfectly, talking about how it wasn't easy to get together but once it happened, and it would happen, it would be explosive.

Then Mike had a drum solo and something completely feral and all-encompassing passed between the two of us. I was done pretending that there was absolutely nothing between us. I just knew that, in the end, one or the both of us would get our world ripped apart and our heart broken, but then there was that little chance that everything would turn out perfectly alright. I wanted to believe in that little chance. I wanted that little chance to expand into something amazing and my worrying to end up being a nonexistent glimmer of doubt.

I felt completely stripped bare and all of my emotions towards this man were being brought to true light. I couldn't hold back another second longer.

This was finally it, the moment that I would give into everything that I had sworn against. The stage lights faded out and the house lights came on but dimmer than before and music began streaming through the strategically placed speakers once the band exited the stage.

I didn't know how long it would be until Mike came out and found me, but I knew without a shadow of a doubt that it would happen.

I left Tessa where she was standing and went to discard my empty glass back at the bar and as soon as I sat the glass on the counter. I felt a light tap on my shoulder and a warm breath at my ear that instantly made a shiver run down my spine, "I bet you could play this song much better on the piano."

I hadn't even noticed that "Faithfully" by Journey had come on through the speakers, I was so into my own head trying to decide the next step between the two of us. I turned around and looked straight into Mike's eyes, the vulnerability and raw passion that was reflecting back at me was enough to take my breath away. He was so unbelievably beautiful, every single bit of him down to his deeply hidden emotional scars. I pulled my bottom lip in between my teeth as he took my hand and led me to the center of the makeshift dance floor.

He pulled me close to where one of his hands was curved around my waist while the other held one of my hands on his chest between us. "Dance with me, Sheridan," he said huskily. It wasn't a request, it was more of a command. You could tell that he was definitely feeling the effects of being so close to me. I wrapped my free hand around his shoulder and rested my chin up on it as we just swayed to the beat of the song.

It really brought a smile to my face whenever he began softly singing the words in my ear while he drew tiny circles on my lower back. I would've never been one to peg Mike for the singing type, but he had a beautiful tone. To hear him sing about being only mine, it almost made me believe it. I closed my eyes and just enjoyed this time that we had being enraptured by the moment.

I could feel eyes on me, so I casually lifted one eye to see Tessa standing in my line of sight with the goofiest grin on her face. I could almost see her shouting to the entire room, "*Told ya so!*" I really wanted to retaliate against her, in a loving way of course, so I mentally gave her the middle finger in a silent fuck you!

The song quickly changed to John Legend. "All of Me" began playing and I leisurely lifted my head so I could lock eyes with him, "What are we doing here, Mike?"

CHAPTER 15

Mike

This night was actually turning out better than anything I had hoped for. Sheridan looked incredible and here she was with me in my arms, where she belonged.

I was honestly expecting her to give me some kind of lip about my bossiness and basically trapping her into dancing with me, but true to Sheridan she surprised me at every single turn.

After the change of songs, I continued to hold her tight, I would've been extremely complacent just standing here all night having the curves of her body in my arms.

She moved her head from my shoulder to look up at me, "What are we doing here, Mike?" Her voice as well as her facial expression was screaming passion and that she was into this moment just as much as I was.

"I'm not entirely sure, but I'd love to find out. Give us tonight," I said as I leaned forward to nuzzle her neck.

I could've kicked the shit out of myself for only offering tonight, but I would worry about the rest later because she eagerly nodded her head affirming my notion to get the hell out of here. I wasn't going to waste another minute.

Releasing her waist, I started lightly pulling her out of the exit but in the end, she sped up her steps and she was almost to the point of pulling me out.

I hoped to hell that I could make it back to my house because the feral feeling I had right now I wanted to take her outside against my truck and there was no way in hell that was happening. I needed to take my time with Sheridan and savor over her every inch.

Once we stepped outside of Emmy Lou's, we were each hit with the muggy summer night air, which did absolutely nothing to cool down our rising temperatures. I didn't expect Sheridan to be so forward until she was shoving me up against the outside of the building and her lips were upon me.

I sent up a slight 'thank you' to the heavens above. I couldn't honestly believe that I was actually having another chance to kiss her because after that one time in the garage I thought that would be it, and it did absolutely nothing to quell my thirst for her.

If rough was what she liked, I was more than happy to oblige. I grabbed her hips in my hands and she wrapped her legs around my waist, then it was my turn to push her up against the building. Her eyes were glazed over and her breathing accelerating. "I have to taste you," I said moments before I nipped her bottom lip then smoothed my tongue over it to dissipate the sting. I began devouring her neck while my hand was massaging her breast through her clothing. My dick had never been so fucking hard, I needed to slow down or run the risk of ending things right here before they ever really began.

I broke apart from her and sat her on her feet, I was out of breath, so in between each rise and fall of my chest, I tried to tell her we had to get home. "Home…" Deep breath. "Now…"

She practically sprinted to my truck, I had never seen her move so quickly. I followed suit and hoisted myself into my seat and fired it up, peeling out of the parking lot. I needed to get home as quickly and safely as possible, I didn't want her to have a change of heart. I hoped to God that wouldn't happen, I still couldn't even believe that we were in this situation.

It was funny to think that just a few months ago I was relieved for the barrier of the center console and now I was cursing the damn thing's existence as it was a hindrance from me touching her.

She seemed to still be holding on, she was currently chewing on a fingernail and fidgeting with her hands, something that I had noticed her do whenever she was nervous, and her feet were resting on my dashboard. Normally I would say something to her, but at this split second she could be completely covered in mud and I wouldn't give a flying fuck about it.

And that's when I knew I was a goner. It hit me like a ton of bricks. I put Sheridan before my beloved truck, I had finally let another woman entirely into my life and into my heart. I took a minute to pray that nothing would mess this up.

I quickly turned onto my street and whipped around the cul-de-sac, slamming on my breaks and skidding to a stop in front of my house.

We were both out of the truck and onto my front porch in a split second. Sheridan had yet to mutter a single word since leaving the bar, I needed to make sure that we were on the same page. I quickly unlocked the door and before I was able to speak a word, she shoved me inside the door and jumped into my arms. I chuckled a bit as I slammed the front door closed with my foot, "So I take it you are still ok with this?"

"Well, if you don't get a move on to your bedroom, I will have some choice words for you. So why the hell are you standing around in your entryway when we could be in your bedroom getting naked?"

She began alternating kissing and nipping my neck, "Well alright then." I didn't waste any more time, I went straight to my bedroom and literally threw Sheridan on my bed. The sound of her giggling as she soared through the air helped me in realizing that this was really happening and I was going to show Sheridan how amazing we would be together. But first I had to take care of a little problem that had been on my heels since entering the house.

I turned towards my open bedroom door and apologized, "I'm sorry Sadie, but you have to stay out," and I quickly shut her out. I had to take a deep breath before I turned around and I was glad that I did. Sheridan was sprawled out on *my* bed. I hadn't ever had another woman in my bed, well not this particular bed, and before that it was only Erin. No, when I had my occasional hookups we always went back to her place, I didn't ever think that I would let another woman into my bed let alone my life, and here was this goddess.

I crawled up the entire length of her body ending on my forearms right above her head and then captured her lips in a slow and sensual kiss. Feeling her hands sink into my hair was incredible and I couldn't even formulate the words to describe it.

Deciding that I had had enough and I was ready to see the rest of her delectable body, I rose from my position and quickly shed free from my clothes, leaving only my boxer briefs as the only article of clothing left on my skin.

She licked her lips and sucked her bottom lip in her mouth again so I knew she definitely liked what she saw.

Kneeling on the bed, I slowly unbuttoned her jeans and lowered the teeth of the zipper one tooth at a time. I practically had to peel the jeans from her body, they were made to look like a second skin. "These jeans are almost as bad as Toby's. I don't know how you can move in them." I completely got them free revealing her glorious legs and a satin red thong which matched the hue of her lips and I proceeded to discard it as well leaving her stark naked from the waist down.

"Do we really have to talk about Toby's jeans *now?*" She sat up and whipped off her tank and threw it on top of my abandoned clothing and her jeans and then unbuttoned the front clasp of her bra, freeing her impressive pert breasts. My mouth watered just looking at them.

A deep guttural growl erupted from my chest and I was back on top of her again, "I wanted to do that. I have often fantasized of taking your clothing off piece by piece, revealing your glorious body."

Taking inventory of all of her curves and features she wasn't just glorious though, "But you are more than just that, you are fucking exquisite, a goddess."

I trailed kisses down her breasts, taking a pink supple nipple into my mouth and giving it a good suck, then releasing it and giving the same attention to the other before I descended my way down the rest of her body.

Placing my mouth on her core, she reacted just the way I'd hoped she would, with her back bowing off of the bed and a string of expletives releasing from her lips as her hands dug into my hair again.

The faster that I licked her pussy and the harder I sucked on her clit, the more response she would give in pulling my hair, so I wasn't exactly gentle in my ravishing of her. I had waited too long to take it easy.

It wasn't until I felt her center begin to tighten around my tongue and her legs begin to tremble I took my mouth off of her, bringing her to the edge, but not quite letting her fall off to the other side. I quickly ditched my boxer briefs and didn't let her get in a protest or a smart ass comment before I slid my straining erection slowly into her tight pussy until I was completely seated.

"Mike!" she screamed digging her nails deep into my back.

Gritting my teeth because it felt so unbelievably amazing,

I began slowly moving bringing my dick out, exposing almost the very tip then thrusting into her quickly again. Each time I completed this I got a little rougher and each time her moans got a little louder and her nails dug in a little further.

I pulled myself completely out and flipped her onto her stomach, she quickly caught on and lifted her ass into the air. I entered her from behind, and this different angle was incredible, I had to refrain from rolling my eyes into the back of my head from the sheer pleasure of it. I bent forward and cradled a breast in my hand, squeezing gently, until she said that one word that made all of the difference.

"Harder!"

Something feral went off inside of me and I started pumping harder and faster and she would push back meeting me thrust for thrust. I decided I wanted to get a bit bold, not knowing how it would come across since she was in such a dark place with Pate, but I was too far gone to turn back now, I lifted my hand and brought it down on her ass. Not too hard, but hard enough for her to feel the bite from the sting. She cried out only to quickly say, "Again!" So who would I be not to comply? I repeated my actions, just a little harder this time and the instant my hand connected with her ass, she screamed out during her release. I had to bite my tongue in order not to come while her pussy was gripping my dick so tightly.

Seeing her ass pink from my handprint turned me on even more. Once her orgasm subsided, I flipped her back over and this time I was going to take my time.

It must've been something about Sheridan, because any other time I wouldn't be able to control my release this long. I wanted to savor this time in case it would be the only time.

Her breathing was still ragged, but I slipped into her once again, this time looking directly in her eyes. And her eyes, God damn those eyes, they were sparkling back up at me and I swear something passed between us right then and there. *She was mine.*

After her second orgasm and me finding my release, I fell onto my back utterly exhausted and without me even asking, she curled into my side. I could tell that things changed for the better and I fell asleep with a smile on my face.

Opening my eyes at the first sight of dawn and hearing the birds chirp outside my window, I sat up and stretched my arms above my head, getting all of the kinks from sleep worked out. I felt completely rested for the first time in years, the same smile that was on my face when I fell asleep still lingered. I didn't think I had ever smiled so much since Hannah had died, in fact, I knew I hadn't. Until I looked down and my smile completely vanished due to the empty space where Sheridan was supposed to be sleeping.

I placed my hand down on the fitted sheet over the mattress expecting to find it still warm, but it was completely cool to the touch.

I wondered if she had a bad dream and just stayed up with Sadie, I would've thought that she would wake me up if it occurred, but I would've have put it past her stubborn self.

I quickly got out of bed and went to my dresser picking out a pair of basketball shorts to slip onto my otherwise naked body. Spotting the pile of clothes on the floor I had to do a double take to confirm that she had indeed taken her clothes off of the pile.

Opening the door, Sadie was right there laying on the hardwood floor, and she perked up whenever she saw my face.

"Morning, Sadie. I'll take you out in a minute. Where is Sheridan, girl?"

Sadie looked at the closed door that was next to mine,

Sheridan's room. I stepped in front of the door and strained to see if I could hear any movement going on from within the room before I turned the knob and slowly opened the door, "Sheridan?"

She was in there alright, snuggled underneath her covers still fast asleep. It made me wonder how long she waited before slipping from my bed. And then I wondered if I had said or done something to make her leave. I thought things had changed, but I guess not.

I felt hurt and betrayed at the thought, but then there would be absolutely no one but myself to blame because I had asked for just one night.

Making a fresh pot of coffee, which wouldn't be strong enough for my present feelings I thought back to my dream last night. I remembered that I told her that I loved her in my dream, whispering it ever so lightly, but what if I actually said that to her not realizing it? I probably scared her off with my forwardness.

A few minutes later I had myself a strong cup of coffee and I sat down at the bar knowing that she would smell the brew and wouldn't be able to resist. Plus she would be getting up for work soon anyways.

Sure enough, she came out covered pretty much from head to toe in her long sleeved bathrobe which practically reached the floor. She went straight to the cabinet to retrieve her favorite coffee mug that said, *Keep Calm I'm A Paramedic.* Which, in fact, was my favorite, but I just let her use it to make her happy, and didn't even spare a second glance my way while filling her cup.

She still hadn't said a word as she retraced her steps back through the living room and evidently down the hallway. I heard the bathroom door shut and the shower turn on and I thought that was just great. I knew a blow off when I saw one. Too bad for her that *her* walk of shame occurred under *my* roof.

I looked down at Sadie who was laying on her side, "You're lucky you have it so easy girl," looked back at the empty space where Sheridan just occupied one last time and let out a long drawn out sigh. "Let's go outside."

By the time Sadie and I had come back in from our lounge session on the back patio, Sheridan had already left for her shift at the diner.

And how lucky for me, Brock wanted to meet at the one place that was crucial for me to avoid...

I let out a loudly audible sigh as I jerked my body into the booth across from Brock at The Diner, and pulled my baseball cap lower over my head to try and shield my eyes. My thought logic was that if I couldn't see her then I wouldn't have to think about her.

Yeah right, who the fuck was I kidding, I had thought of very little else except her since she made her grand appearance in Brown County.

"What the hell crawled up your ass?" Brock hissed my way as he then proceeded to take a drink from his water.

"I really don't want to talk about it. I tried to call to get you to change the location or at least cancel my coming here, but *someone* wouldn't answer the damn phone."

"Yeah..." He raised his finger pointing it towards my face, "You know, I had a feeling that was what you were trying to call for, which is exactly why I didn't answer." He said matter of fact. Lowering his hand, he started dragging his fingers through the condensation on his glass. "Tessa thought it'd be great to be a little spy last night and followed you and Sheridan out of the bar and saw you two all over each other. So I wanted to hear about what went on last night."

My brows arched and if my hat wasn't pulled down so low, you would've seen that they reached my hairline. "I call bullshit."

"Alright," he said raising both hands in a mock surrender, "I could really care less that you and Sheridan finally succumbed to the inevitable, but if I came home later without any ounce of gossip to feed to my wife, she might physically combust. Plus it was the only way to get to come here, she caught wind that I was coming to this grease trap. You know how she's been on my ass about eating healthier." Slapping a hand on his belly, he continued, "Apparently I'm starting to form a gut." I wasn't about to step into that trap, so I just kept my mouth shut.

"And I'm guessing by the way you keep readjusting your hat lower over your face and the way that Sheridan is ignoring your presence whenever she passes by our table, but is peeking through the window in the kitchen, so you can't see, that things didn't go well."

I quickly turned around only to find the small circle window that was on the door to the kitchen completely empty.

My shoulders slumped as I turned back to face Brock, a stony expression darkening my face, I felt truly defeated. "I thought things went well. When I woke up this morning she was back in her own bed asleep and then completely ignored me once she woke up." I wasn't going to confess to him of my mental freak out. I was supposed to be a man dammit, I didn't like all of these extra feelings. I continued to wrack my brain at what could have caused her awkward brushoff. She couldn't be embarrassed because of her reaction to my spanking her, could she? Maybe I'll never know.

CHAPTER 16

Sheridan

As I stood flush against the cool tile of the kitchen wall with a hand on my chest, my heart was frantically beating against my ribcage at the possibility of getting caught staring after Mike. I realized how ridiculous I looked especially when I glanced up and saw Archie staring at me with one raised eyebrow and his arms crossed with his spatula sticking out. If I wasn't mentally freaking out about the mess, I was in I would've almost laughed at his expression. Archie and serious weren't really two things that went well together.

I really didn't want to explain myself and my actions especially to Archie, so I took a defensive stance and said, "I'm taking a break," and quickly exited the restaurant through the backdoor.

Once I was out of the confines of the muggy kitchen, the sultriness outside wasn't much better but at least I wasn't in the same occupied space as Mike at the moment. I needed to get my head together because Mike Jameson was definitely clouding my judgment.

I leaned my entire body up against the aluminum of the

diner and closed my eyes. I was beginning to wonder if staying in Brown County was even going to be possible after what happened last night. Don't get me wrong, I greatly wanted it to happen, but feelings got in the way and now it has ruined everything.

After being with Mike last night, I was deliciously spent, I had never known that sex could be so amazing and I could feel so incredibly wanted. I guess what was different is that I was actually wanting to be a part of it. I immediately curled into Mike's side and was ready for a great night's sleep being in his embrace. That was until his breathing quickly evened out as he fell into a deep sleep and then he muttered four little words that would any other time make my heart flutter. "I love you, Sheridan." He loved *me.* Of course, I completely reciprocated those feelings, but it just wasn't in the cards for us.

I didn't waste any time slipping from his clutches and from his bed, immediately missing the close, intimate contact with him. I couldn't allow myself to be happy and sleep with him when we couldn't be together and make it work, especially because of…

The backdoor to the diner slammed open and Wanda appeared, "Sheridan we are getting pretty crowded in there. Normally I wouldn't say anything, but you've been out here for twenty minutes. I also needed to check to make sure you were alright."

Shit. I couldn't believe that I was abusing company time while reminiscing of things that could've been. "I'm so sorry Wanda, my mind is just elsewhere today. I'll go in right away." I hurried and bypassed her on my way back in and immediately went to introduce myself to the customer not even sparing a second glance at Mike on my way.

"Welcome to The Diner, can I get you something to drink?" Then I looked up from my notepad and realized that I actually knew who it was. "Maggie?"

She glanced up from her menu and gave me a surprised look before quickly recovering, "Oh my goodness, Sheridan, how are you?"

I couldn't help the infectious grin that spread across my face at all that had changed in my life, for the better, and most of it was because of Mike. Wasn't that a kick in the heart?

"I'm doing good, just got my cast off a few weeks ago." Maggie followed my gaze down to my ankle as I pointed my foot and began rotating it around in a circle.

"I had absolutely no clue that you were still in Brown County."

"Yeah, I decided to stay, I'm actually living in Mike's spare bedroom, but hopefully that won't be for much longer." My expression turned into one of guilt. Why had we given into each-others desires and ruined everything? Would our friendship ever recover from this? "I'm looking for my own place. And I've been working here for about five or six weeks now, I love it. I love being able to work." Just the thought of having a job and my own money put a smile back on my face. I wouldn't ever have to answer to anyone ever again.

We conversed for a few minutes as I was able in between bringing out her drink and pancakes which basically almost had her eyes rolling in the back of her head over her sheer enjoyment of eating them. If I hadn't known any better, I would think that she was pregnant.

When she had finally finished her entire plate, I seriously thought that if no one was looking she would've licked all of the existing syrup clean from her plate, she walked up to the counter to pay for her meal.

The bell above the door dinged, and he was right on time.

"Good morning, Sheriff," I said to Charlie. He came in just about every morning and ordered the same exact thing, the big breakfast platter to go. Sometimes if I wasn't too busy I would go ahead and put in his order so it would be ready and waiting for him so he wouldn't have to spend too long in here.

"Good morning, Sheridan, Maggie," he said while he looked longingly at Maggie, never taking his eyes off of her. Hmm…perhaps she was the reason why he always looked so sad all the time. I really hadn't known him long, but I could just tell that something just hadn't seemed right with him lately.

"Hi," Maggie finally croaked out after several seconds of just standing there looking dumbfounded. Then the poor thing started to look sick and she covered her mouth and darted off in the direction of the bathroom. Too many pancakes I suppose, or was she really pregnant?

"Does she come in here often?" Charlie asked. He almost seemed a bit hopeful at the aspect of possibly running into her here again.

I remorsefully shook my head in the negative and said, "No, this is the first time I've seen her since my accident."

I ran to the kitchen to get his usual breakfast to go and brought it back to him, took his money, and he was out the door with only a solemn look exchanged between us.

Poor guy.

The crowd had diminished quite a bit so I went to the restroom to check and make sure that Maggie was alright. I knew she was a nurse, but it never hurt to lend an open ear, especially when I owed Maggie so much after my accident. I felt sad that I hadn't ever called Maggie after she visited me while I was still in the hospital following my wreck. Was I so wrapped up in myself and Mike that I couldn't have taken the time to call Maggie and at least thank her? That wasn't the type of person that I was and definitely not who I wanted to be.

I lightly knocked on the door to the women's restroom before I poked my head in, "Are you ok sweetie?" I was truly concerned for her because she looked extremely pained. And I didn't think it was because she had just finished getting sick.

"Yeah, I'm fine. Is uh…is Charlie still out there?" she

stuttered but finally asked.

I pushed open the door and came all the way into the restroom with Maggie. "No, Sheriff Hennings comes in every morning to pick up his breakfast to take it back to the station." I went to get a paper towel and run it underneath the cool water of the faucet before handing it to Maggie so she could cool and wipe down her face. "I remembered you two were together when you helped me after my wreck. Apparently that isn't the case anymore?"

I didn't mean to be so forward, but it just made my heart hurt from both of them looking so incredibly sad all of the time. All she could do was shake her head, "no."

"Then that's why he always looks sad when he comes in. Makes just enough small talk with the customers so they don't think he's rude, since he's new to the badge and all."

Her face seemed to fall even more so after my explanation and I almost regretted giving her so much information to how he always acted. It was absolutely none of my business and here I was putting my nose in it like a nosey Nancy.

We both retreated out of the bathroom and I immediately stopped in my tracks because right in front of me was Mike.

There seemed to be some sort of staring contest happening between the two of us. I wanted so badly to apologize or say something regarding my actions, but I couldn't muster up enough courage let alone formulate the words that needed to be said.

His expression was first one of pain before it abruptly became extremely heated. I couldn't help the way mine morphed to end up looking just like his. I wanted him again, but I just couldn't. I could physically see the lust radiating off of him in waves, and I knew that he wouldn't be the first person to walk away, so I had to do it. I reverted my gaze to the floor and I skirted around him, not saying a word and went about doing my job.

I walked into a dimly lit house and even Sadie didn't run up to give me her usual doggie kisses so I assumed her and Mike were out in the tropical oasis, also known as his glorious backyard. Relaxing on his hammock sounded heavenly after the long day I've had, but I couldn't bear to be directly around him right now, and it wouldn't be fair for me to be either.

Wanda wanted me to work overtime, which normally wouldn't be a problem, but after the events of last night and today had unfolded I was just mentally exhausted. A long hot shower and bed would be more of my speed for tonight.

I went to the kitchen so I could retrieve a bottle of water from the fridge before I disappeared for the night and I had to stop and gasp by the scene that was before me. I could see Mike in the backyard from out his bay window, but the way he had his head dropped down and cradled in his hands made my heart split in two. I was to blame for his anguish and I hated that more than anything. Last night should have never happened even though I really couldn't bring myself to regret it, quite the contrary, it'll be something that I always hold near and dear to my heart. There were just things that Mike didn't and couldn't understand, and being kept in the dark about them, for now, was what was best for the both of us.

The shrill sound of my mother's ringtone startled me out of my longing preoccupation. Opening my phone, I still hadn't been able to afford to be brought into the new age of smart phone technology, I was extremely lucky enough as it was to have a flip phone, I pressed the answer button, "Hey, mama." I was only able to get out those two words before my mother broke out into hysterics on the other line.

My stomach completely bottomed out and I felt as if the

walls were rapidly closing in all around me. I had no idea what was going on yet, but just the sound of her sobbing had me instantly in fear and thrown into a panic attack.

My lungs had seized to bring in any additional oxygen and my heart was racing a mile a minute, but not in the positive way it would whenever I saw Mike. I could hear my mother finally calm down enough to repeat my name over and over, but I couldn't bring in any air in order to be able to answer her.

I felt extremely weak and it wasn't long until my legs gave out from underneath me and I fell to the tiled floor of Mike's kitchen. I was wheezing and I couldn't even formulate a sound to get Mike's attention.

I noticed brown fur in front of my face and realized that Sadie must have come in through the doggy door and she vanished as quickly as she appeared. Moments later Mike came rushing into the house, no doubt in a panic after seeing me lying limp on the floor.

"Sheridan," he fell to his knees beside me and quickly enveloped my into his embrace, absolutely no questions asked. He held my back to his front and he whispered softly and soothingly into my ear, "I've got you, sweetheart. Everything will be just fine you just need to relax. Take a deep breath in, and now let it out."

After a few minutes, my heart rate and breathing returned back to normal and I noticed that Mike was rubbing his fingertips up and down my arm. I wanted so badly to relax into his embrace and just enjoy being in his arms, but I remembered that my mother was hopefully still waiting on the line.

I dove forward to retrieve my cell phone that had fallen with me to the floor but was still luckily intact, a good thing about the old phones, they were much tougher. "Mama, are you still there?" Hearing her confirmation, I delved right into apologizing, "Oh mama, I'm so sorry."

"Sheridan don't worry about it," her voice was still

cracking as if she was going to break again at any moment. "Sheridan, it's your dad."

Another gasp left my mouth and I tried my very best to remain calm, it helped that I was still within the confines of Mike's grasp and he held onto me tightly, while the rest of my mother's news unfolded.

I hung up the phone after getting all the information on the situation and I was utterly helpless at what I should do.

"What's going on, sweetheart?" Mike whispered in my ear again sending butterflies flying through my stomach. I didn't have time to be lustful, I needed to find a way to get to my dad.

I quickly stood up from my position on Mike's lap and turned around to see him following suit. "My dad is in the hospital, he had a massive heart attack. I have to find a way to get to him."

I was quickly trying to calculate how much it would be to take a cab back home, or better yet, a bus. Being four hours away, a bus would be much cheaper, and that was one thing I didn't have in abundance to spend, money. But if it was to get to my dad, money would be no object.

I walked towards my bedroom so I could change out of my uniform when I placed my hand on the doorknob to my room, Mike's hand appeared over the top of mine.

"Sheridan, don't be silly. I would be more than happy to take you to your dad."

Tears welled up in my eyes as I looked up at him, but they weren't for the reasons that Mike was probably thinking. I was absolutely grateful that he volunteered to take me, but I didn't really know how to explain to him certain aspects of my life.

CHAPTER 17

Mike

Sheridan was seriously worrying me. After she relentlessly tried and then failed at talking me out of taking her to see her father in the hospital, she had completely shut down. Walking in to see her in the middle of a panic attack, it definitely scared the shit out of me. But instantly my paramedic training kicked in and I made her relax and soothingly talked her through it. It was incredibly nice to hold her in my arms once again, even though she wasn't physically aware of it. It was a stomp on the foot once she darted up off of my lap.

We were now right outside of Atlanta with almost two hours to go. She apparently grew up about four hours east of Brown County in an even smaller town, but now her parents lived even further away from Atlanta.

I almost wondered if she thought that we would run into Pate, but I knew that wouldn't be a possibility since he lived nowhere near them now.

Sheridan didn't have much information to go on just that

her father had a heart attack and with his underlying heart condition any more abuse on his heart couldn't be good news.

I spared a glance her way to see her biting her nails again, telling me that she was nervous, but this time she had added a slight rocking motion to where she wasn't still in her seat.

I couldn't stand the silent treatment any longer, I pounded my fists on the steering wheel and yelled out the first thing that came to mind. "Why did you leave me last night?"

She stopped her rocking and took her fingers away from her mouth and just stared at me incredulously. She began fidgeting even more as she averted her gaze from mine. And just when I thought that she wasn't going to say anything, she started explaining. "Listen, I had an incredible time with you last night," I felt a glimmer of hope spark within my chest, until she said the inevitable ending word, "but… I just figured that it would be awkward for us if I had stayed." Shrugging her shoulders as if it wasn't any big deal.

I knew she was lying, I could just tell by her failure to meet my eyes even for a split second when I sparred a moment to look from the road.

"Awkward for who, you? Because it wouldn't have been the least bit awkward for me. I know I said just one night, but I believe that last night proved that we could be amazing together, if you would just let it. I haven't opened my heart to anyone in many years, so you have to know that I'm not just throwing this around. All of these feelings aren't usual for me. And I…really care about you, Sheridan." I tried to grab for her hand that was resting upon her lap, but she moved it at the last moment.

"Mike, you wouldn't be saying those things if you knew…" She trailed off apparently expecting me to fill in the blanks. I wasn't a fucking mind reader.

"If I knew what?! Just fucking tell me already Sheridan!" I knew I had been a bit too harsh when I saw a single tear slide down her cheek and she turned to where she was looking out the window at the world passing by.

We rushed into the hospital after parking my truck and she quickly bypassed the information desk as if she knew exactly where she was going. Her mother must have told her the room number because she didn't stop until she was right outside of a hospital room.

"Ok, thank you for bringing me here, Mike." She continued to fiddle with her hands and she still wouldn't look at me but kept looking at the closed door to the private room.

"Sheridan, I'm not going anywhere," I went to place my hand under her chin to get her to look at me but a look of pure fear came over her face as the door to the hospital room opened.

A woman who appeared to be in her middle fifties appeared in the doorway and she was the spitting image of Sheridan, just a little older and with graying hair.

"Sheridan, honey I thought that I heard your voice out here."

The fearful look on Sheridan's face had yet to dissipate and I was seriously beginning to wonder what in the world she had to be afraid of. A few seconds later, I had my answer. And that fucking answer hit me square in the solar plexus, knocking the wind completely out of me.

A set of tiny fingers grasped the bottom of the heavy wooden door and started opening it once again. And a little raven haired boy with amazing green eyes hidden behind a pair of glasses appeared.

He stared up at me before looking towards Sheridan and breaking out into a humungous grin.

Those eyes and that hair. I fucking knew those eyes.

I looked at Sheridan and she gave me a worried grin as

she slumped her shoulders.

If it wasn't confirmed by just the looks of the little boy, the moment when he screeched, "Mommy!" and jumped into her outstretched arms did.

My heart immediately sank and I stumbled back a step as if I had been hit square in the chest as the entirety of the situation hit me head on. *This* was what she was hiding? It wasn't just a *something* it was a fucking *someone!* Sheridan had a *son* and didn't tell me. She didn't tell *me.* Here I had been falling in love with a woman who now seemed like a complete stranger to me, all in the blink of an eye.

What in the actual fuck?

I yanked my hat off of my head, my constant reminder of what I had lost in my life and drug my now sweaty hand through my hair, tugging on the ends. Pain was what I needed to feel instead of this constant despair. I wondered if I could find a concrete wall to punch, hell I was in a hospital full of them. But somewhere in the recesses of my mind I thought it would be frowned upon especially for a paramedic to punch a wall within a hospital.

I jerked my body away from the group not even caring that I came off as a complete and utter asshole to Sheridan's mom and started retreating back down the corridor in which we just came through moments earlier. This wasn't something you kept from someone.

My steps were hasty and if it seemed like I was stomping like a kid who didn't get their way, then that was too fucking bad.

The pressure from a hand on my shoulder had me immediately swinging around. I was incredibly defensive and I dared anyone to mess with me especially now.

Sheridan looked distraught and for a moment I was glad that she looked how I felt. Shifting from foot to foot, the guilt seeped from her pores.

"I'm sorry, Mike."

That was it? That was all she had to say to me?

I stared at the woman who I now regretfully loved and I honestly didn't know who she was anymore. I was waiting for a further explanation that apparently wasn't coming.

"You're sorry? What are you sorry that you didn't tell me you had a son, or you're sorry that I found out?"

"His name is Benjamin," she twisted her hands together and turned to look back down the hall at the little boy who was still waiting for her. "The reasoning that I never mentioned him is *my* business." She pointed to her chest and tears were now welling up in her eyes and her voice cracked when she spoke. "I tried to stay away from you, I tried not to get close because of this very reason. I didn't want anyone to get hurt."

"You didn't want anyone to get hurt?" I responded sarcastically. This whole situation was beyond disbelief. "Well, how is that working out for you?"

She gasped and I could tell that I had her exactly where I wanted to. I hoped that the knife was putting enough pressure on her heart just as it was mine.

"I'll get you a bus ticket back to Brown County, I'll be going out of town for a few days. In the meantime, I want your shit out of my house!" I yelled sternly, cutting my hand through the air trying to make a point that she messed with the wrong man, and not even giving a shit that my voice was carrying down the hallway.

My hardened exterior was quickly put back in place as I left Sheridan and my empty heart behind in that hospital hallway.

I failed myself and my original vow. Why had I volunteered to take in a raven haired goddess who ended up being exactly what I had speculated. A man-eater.

I really didn't know where I was going to end up until I was on the outskirts of Wentzville, the suburb of St. Louis where I grew up.

I knew what I needed to do, but I really didn't know if I would be welcome in my parents' home. I hadn't been back or barely even spoken to my father in the three and a half years it'd been since I'd moved to Brown County.

Things hadn't changed much as I navigated my way around town. I stopped by Jameson Auto first to see if my dad was piddling around under the hood of a vehicle but what I saw was a closed shop. And by the looks of it, it had been vacant for some time now.

I jumped down out of my truck and walked around the lot, kicking stray rocks with my boot that inhabited the place. Piles of used, worn out tires cluttered the parking lot and weeds had grown up through the cracks in the pavement. There were cracks in the concrete?! My dad wouldn't ever fail on the upkeep of the shop, it was his pride and joy. He loved being here and being able to help fix everyone's vehicles. My dad liked being depended on, thrived from it actually.

What had happened to the shop? It worried me that my dad never tried to contact me to let me know about the status of the shop. But then again I never ever really gave him the resources to be able to contact me. What kind of son have I been to not even let my own father know where I lived? The kind that was shutting everyone and everything out.

Pulling up in front of my childhood home nothing really seemed amiss on this aspect. The yard was neatly trimmed with colorful flowers filling all of the beds, just like my ma had it every year.

Sitting in my truck just looking at the place that was always home up until the last several years, the dread of my father's reaction to my being here was gnawing at me. It was almost to the point where I just wanted to take off and not even show my shameful face to him, but I had already trekked this far, might as well face the music sometime or another.

Just when I was going to stall myself for a few more minutes, not being able to muster up the courage to even connect my knuckles to the door, I looked back up at the front porch to see my father leaning against the railing that attached to the house, arms crossed in front of his chest with his stern, parent-like expression on his face. It was the face that I remembered getting whenever I was in trouble, which didn't happen all that often growing up. But whenever I was on the receiving end of that look I knew not to mess around.

I took a deep breath and let it out hoping that it would alleviate some of my nerves, but if anything it just made it worse. I couldn't believe that here I was a grown ass man and I was afraid of what my father would say to me.

I pulled the bill to my ball cap down, lowering it over my face so my dad couldn't see all of the dishonorable guilt that consumed me and got out of my truck, with slow movements. *Why had I waited so long to come back here?*

I knew the answer, Hannah wasn't here so there was absolutely no reason for me to be.

I saw my dad release an impatient sigh as he turned around to re-enter his house.

It felt weird stepping back over the threshold, but looking around it was as if I had never left. Absolutely nothing had changed, he even still had it the same as it was when my ma was still alive. That was how opposed to change my father was, which just further reiterated my confusion with the shop.

I stuffed my hands into the pockets of my worn out jeans and saw that my dad had taken up his usual seat in his old La-Z-

Boy recliner. "What happened to the shop?" I muttered half underneath my breath.

"Boy, sit your ass down," his voice boomed throughout the living room. I had forgotten just how loud my father's voice had projected.

I took my hands out of my pockets and let my arms hang down my side as my shoulders slumped forward. I was time warped right back into tenth grade whenever my father got mad at me for sneaking out. I said that I didn't get in trouble much growing up even though I snuck out...

All. The. Time.

You just had to know how to *not* get caught. The one time I did, I felt that backlash weeks later as I was grounded for that long.

Most kids got their electronics taken away, but I wasn't much on modern day devices. No, I got my toolbox taken away. My father knew exactly how to sock-it to me where it counted the most.

I did as my father instructed and planted my ass on the old couch that my mother had picked out during my freshman year of high school. I remembered it had been that long because this was, in fact, the same couch that I had lost my virginity on that summer. Memories that weren't necessarily good ones now though.

I rested my forearms on my knees and leaned forward, trying to somewhat brace myself for what was going to come next.

Just looking at my dad, I could tell that he's aged a great deal in the three and a half years it's been since I've seen him. His hair was thinning out and the gray was much more prominent than it had been. He had even lost quite a bit of weight, he actually looked quite fit, not frail like I would've pictured since he has lost some weight. But it was his eyes that held the most change, he didn't really look all that sad. There was almost the twinkle back in his eyes that he had lost after my mother passed away. He almost looked…happy, content, satisfied even.

"You've met someone," I said looking him directly in his eyes. I almost missed the small flutter of guilt pass over him.

"I was about to say the same thing to you, son," he looked down at his lap, where he had one foot resting across his other knee. "Mike, it really has been too long."

And that was all it took for my proverbial dam of emotions to break. For the next three hours, he told me all about how he sold Jameson Auto because it had just become too much for just himself and he couldn't trust anyone to do exceptional work on vehicles since I had left. So he retired and took up running, which I really got a kick out of because my father was never really much of a runner, but now that explained the toned look and his weight loss. Then he told me of meeting Sandra, she was a few years younger than him, and it turned out she was also my Sophomore English Teacher. Remembering back to when I had Mrs. Westmore, I always thought that she was a looker, for a somewhat older woman of course, so I didn't give my dad too hard of a time. It also helped that he told me that no one could ever replace his first and only true love; my mother, but he really enjoyed Sandra's company.

"Now that I've done all of the talking, it's your turn to spill. What the hell have you been up to and what is her name?"

I gave him a true, honest grin.

"You know it's nice to see you smiling again," I saw a tear form in the crease of my father's eye, I had never seen him cry very often, so it really took me aback. "You weren't the only one who lost someone, Mike. I lost my only grandchild and then six months later your mother, and during all of that time, I lost you as well. When you went through the depression, I never thought you would come out of it, I was so worried about you. I tried and tried for you to get help, but you didn't hear me, you wouldn't. The underlying guilt of everything totally took over everything. You drank your way through those six months and I'm really sorry to say this, but I'm surprised it didn't kill you."

"I know, dad. So many times I thought about killing myself so I could be with Hannah, but I knew that she ultimately wouldn't want that. One day it was like a switch, as hard to believe as that is. I just woke up and knew that I had to start over, although I really didn't start anything over. I just moved to Brown County and threw myself into several different things, but keeping to myself the majority of the time. I'm a drummer in a band, we play a few gigs every now and again. I also work on cars on the side, and I became a paramedic. I now know that my mission in life is to save lives."

I looked up at my dad and seeing the pride written all over his face was exactly the reaction that I had missed seeing from him. I knew that I was doing something right in my life now.

"Now, that answers one part of my question, what about the other?"

I had tried my damnedest to not mention Sheridan, but I could tell that my father wasn't going to let this go.

I swallowed past the lump that had formed in my throat at the thought of Sheridan and my hasty decision to leave her behind with only a bus ticket to get herself back to Brown County. That wasn't me, that wasn't the man that I was. I almost felt ashamed to tell him what I had done, but just her deceit did me in.

"Her name is Sheridan and I love her. But I just found out purely by accident that she has been hiding a son from me. She knew my standpoint on not having any more children, so she just lied to me by not telling me." I went on to tell him how I met Sheridan and about her past and our friendship. That she was the first woman that I had let into my life and my heart since Erin and Hannah. How she cracked through my shell and taught me how to love again.

"So let me get this straight, you left her with a bus ticket back to Brown County because you found out that she had a son? But you also said that she's had to change her last name because she is running from an ex-boyfriend? And also that you never knew where she was from until you went to take her to the hospital?"

"I still don't know where she is from, her parents had moved to a different town after she had moved out of her house after high school, but yes that's the gist of it."

He rested his hand up underneath his chin in a movement that I always used to call his thinking stance. "I don't know the whole story but it seems to me that she hid her son from you because she was hiding her son from everyone. She has basically been continuously running from a horrible man, so she didn't mention her son because she was trying to keep *him* safe. You are just like your momma, boy, always jumping to conclusions."

I gave him a snort, my way of a dismissive laugh, he was talking about my ma and I was going to begin to get defensive. He pointed to my facial expression and chuckled, "See what I mean, again you just jumped to some imaginary conclusion. You didn't take the time to find out what I meant, you instantly were ready to react and attack. I didn't mean anything bad by being just like your mother, but it's true, she was never one to be patient and always jumped to conclusions." He stood from his recliner and came over to have a seat next to me on the couch.

"You know you said that your mission in life was to save lives because you couldn't save Hannah's?" I looked down at my hands that I had clasped in front of me and swallowed loudly and nodded my head. "I believe this Sheridan has saved your life as well, don't you?"

I sat there just letting his words seep in. I never really thought of it that way, but I supposed he was right. Who knew what kind of path I was ultimately leading myself down? I still had the occasional drink, but it wasn't as profusely as before my move, so I wasn't too concerned with major depression again, but who could predict those instances? Without Sheridan, who knew if I would've actually ever let someone else in? And as much as I didn't want to admit it, he was completely one hundred percent correct in the aspect of me jumping to conclusions. I immediately get up on my haunches and retaliate, asking questions later which wasn't any way to live my life.

But now I've gone off on Sheridan and told her to get out of my home and more or less my life. Would she completely move out of Brown County? What could I do to make it right?

"Don't think I don't see those wheels turning in your head. You may have to wait awhile for wounds to settle and heal a little, but when the time comes you'll know what to do to make things right with her."

Now it was time for me to think about the other hindrance, her son.

"How could I ever replace Hannah though? I don't know if I have it in my heart to be a father to Benjamin." I knew that Sheridan was no longer able to have children, everything made sense now. How she skirted around different topics and the constant phone calls with her mom. Who knew if I'll ever have the chance to know the entire story?

"Now Mike, whoever told you that you had to replace Hannah? Did Sheridan?"

"Well, no."

"There is absolutely no replacing her. She will continue to hold a special place in your heart, same as she does mine. But that doesn't mean that you should completely shut yourself out to the idea of having more kids. Do you remember how much joy she brought you and how much fun you used to have together? Why would you want to deny yourself that joy again? You said that Hannah wouldn't have wanted you to kill yourself just so you could be with her, don't you think that she would want you to have more kids so you could have that again?"

He stood up and walked to the fireplace where a picture of Hannah and I together was perched on the mantle and removed it from its place. Holding it in his hand, he smiled at her chubby little face. I remembered the day that picture was taken very well, it was the same day she gave me my hat; my birthday. She wanted to help me blow out my candles and thought it'd be funny to smear icing all over my face, so I did the same to her. My mom was all about taking pictures and she didn't hesitate in snapping our icing clad faces, capturing that special memory.

"Son, I knew that for you being a father was the best thing in the world and you were amazing at it, I mean look who you had for a role model." That little joke caused me to lift up a corner of my mouth in a small grin, but it also accomplished lightening the mood in the room a little. And in all honesty, I had two exceptional role models and I was so thankful for them, which reiterated another reason why I had been such a dick to stay away all these years.

I really needed to do some thinking about if I would actually be able to open my heart up for another child.

"Bottom line, I know you blame yourself since you weren't there for Hannah, but Erin should have. I really want to say that it was no one's fault, but I believe in my heart that if Erin was in a better place then she would've fought hell and earth for your little girl."

I ended up spending a few days with my father, it was nice to catch up on old times and I even got to see him interact with Sandra. I had called Brock in the meantime and gave him somewhat of a vague explanation as to what was going on without giving away too many details. It wasn't anyone else's business but mine and Sheridan's. But he was there to check on Sadie if Sheridan really did take my eviction to heart.

I was thinking back to the last thing my dad told me before I left his house. The screen door was propped open on his arm as he stood there watching me walk down the sidewalk towards my truck. He hollered out causing me to stop and listen, "When you get her back be sure to bring by the woman who brought my son back to life so I can properly thank her."

I honestly didn't know how to respond to that so I just shook my head and kept on following the sidewalk towards my truck.

Walking into my house, Sadie immediately met me at the door and was jumping with excitement to see me after a few days. I had no way of knowing whether Sheridan had come and gone, but the atmosphere within my home seemed different.

I made it as far as the living room before I looked down at my chocolate lab and crouched down on my haunches to rub her head, "Where is Sheridan, Sadie Belle?" Even her nickname had stuck with me.

She immediately began whining and whimpering leading me to Sheridan's closed bedroom door. She sat down and lifted a paw to scratch on the wooden door and then leaned forward and sniffed at the gap underneath it.

My heart was racing because Sadie had never really acted like this before, so I didn't know what to expect when I turned the brass knob. The bed was completely made and the top of the dresser was completely free of any of Sheridan's belongings. It looked as if she had never even been here.

I rushed out of her room and across the hall stopping at the doorframe to the bathroom. Without even switching the light on, I could tell all of her hair products that had cluttered my countertop were removed.

The finality of it all hit me like a ton of bricks.

Subconsciously aware that I was stumbling to my kitchen, my heart was ripping even more in two. I had no idea where she went or even if she was still in Brown County. All because I jumped to hasty inexcusable conclusions.

I braced my hands on the edge of the counter and glanced down to see my favorite coffee mug and hers, washed and waiting next to the coffee maker with a post-it note laying partly underneath that just said, "Thanks."

I removed it from the granite, feeling the thin yellow paper between my fingertips. This could possibly be the last thing that I could ever have of Sheridan.

HAPTER 18

Sheridan

I stood stock still in the middle of the hallway watching Mike's retreating form until I could no longer see his image. I was truly defeated and just wanted to curl up into a ball and cry. He didn't even give me time to explain why I hid Ben from him. It was something that I wasn't proud of, but I would do anything to protect my child, which wasn't something I could say about Mike's ex-wife.

I slowly turned around towards the direction of my mother and Ben, and I had to muster up enough strength to not give into my emotions. I felt emotionally and physically drained and it was my own fault. I knew that I trusted Mike with my entire life, didn't I trust him with Ben's as well?

I guess that it was the fact that no one other than my parents knew what had happened to Ben. After I had found out that I was pregnant again, I didn't want the same outcome to occur with this baby as it did with my last because of Pate's actions, so I got out of there. When I told Mike that those eleven months were the best of my life, I wasn't kidding. I had a healthy, beautiful baby boy to call my own. But when Pate had found me that one day that I went to the grocery store I had to come up with some sort of plan. I was able to sign over all of my parental rights to my parents without anyone the wiser.

I would call when I could to checkup on Ben and I knew that someday I would be able to bring him back into my home and not have to worry with looking over my shoulder every five seconds to see if Pate had found me. Which was why I got so content and comfortable with Mike, he wouldn't hesitate to protect me at a moment's notice.

How had I ended up going back with Pate you ask? Lack of bravery to stand up to him and the fact of the matter that he threatened to kill my parents if I didn't. Pate Strickland wasn't someone that you wanted to mess with, I knew that firsthand, so I wasn't going to risk anything happening to Ben or my parents.

So yeah, I kept Ben a secret, but it was my ultimate sacrifice as a mother.

Returning back to my family I was so excited to see my baby Ben, but I had wished that the circumstances could have been a little different.

His mouth curved up in the biggest grin and he ran and jumped back into my open arms, "Mommy!" he squealed. "I missed you so much!" I curled my arms around him as he clung to my neck. I wanted to squeeze him tight and never let him go, and hopefully soon I would have enough resources to do just that. But now with Mike kicking me out, I was pushed back to square one. I had money set back that I had saved, so I almost had enough for the security deposit on an apartment and the first month's rent, but that didn't help me on the furniture. I really didn't know if Brown County had a used furniture store, I really didn't know much about the town at all except for being cooped up in Mike's house and The Diner.

I felt Ben's clammy little hands on my cheeks as he squeezed them together trying to get my attention. I had spaced out stressing about my living situation, which needs to be placed in the back of my mind for now since I was with Ben.

"How is my Benji? Are you being such a good boy for Mamaw and Papaw?"

"Yes, Mommy," he finally let go of my cheeks but not before he gave me an Eskimo kiss, rubbing our noses together. This was how he loved giving kisses. "Papaw is sick," he told me through a frown.

"I know, pumpkin, let's go see Papaw." I placed him on his feet, making sure he had his bearings before fully letting him go and he grabbed ahold of my hand.

Leaving him with my parents was one of the hardest things that I've ever had to endure while being a mother, even above everything I've went through with Pate. Not being able to soothe him through his nightmares or taking him to get his first pair of prescription glasses. He was only three, so he may not remember not being with me, but it was forever engraved in my conscience.

I think that was another reason why I was so hesitant to tell Mike about Benjamin, he is currently the same age that Hannah was whenever she died. I knew he could guestimate his age and even though Ben was tall for his age, he still looked and acted like your average typical three year old.

I was extremely lucky that Ben was still young enough to where he wasn't resentful for me not being around. My mother was so good about including me when telling him bedtime stories and showing him pictures of me to remind him who I was since I wasn't able to be around very often. I did talk to him on the phone every single chance that I got.

My heart was extremely heavy leaving Ben once again, but once my dad went through the process of having a stint put in to alleviate some of the blockage, I had to be on my way once again.

Apparently someone from up above was looking out for me because no sooner had I returned to Mike's house to pack up my belongings I received a phone call from Maggie Walker asking if I wanted to sublet on her apartment. She knew that I was looking for my own space and she was moving out of Brown County for reasons she didn't divulge, but she assured me that it was alright with her landlord so I didn't hesitate on snatching it up. The best part was that she was leaving it fully furnished. I only had to bring Ben's bed and his belongings and this could be home.

It had been only a few days since I'd been living in Maggie's apartment and I really just felt rather lonely. My mom thought that I needed to at least have a fully functioning vehicle before I brought Ben to live with me and I really had to agree. Even though Maggie had left me her car because she was going to find a new place to move, in the end she didn't end up leaving Brown County. So I no longer had use of her car. I was worried there about a minute because I was afraid I was going to be back to square one on my living situation, but Maggie assured me that she wouldn't do that to me. She ended up moving in with Sheriff Hennings. She even sold me what was left of the furniture she didn't want for an insanely good price. It was nice to see someone get their happy ever after even if I wouldn't ever get mine.

But that's alright, I didn't need a man in my life. A fear free life with Ben was all that I could want or need.

I was going to be a little early for my shift at The Diner, but I was bored at home and my mind would wander back to

Mike. I really needed to call Brock at the shop and see how much longer my car would be. I really would've thought that it'd be finished by now. I had no idea when Mike would be back into town and I really didn't think that seeing me would be on top of his list, so hopefully Brock would know what was up.

I fiddled with my keys locking up my apartment and stuck inside of my own head that I didn't see anyone or anything else in this case in the hallway. I turned around and almost ran right into a rolling piano.

"Ouch," I said, not really knowing why because I didn't actually run into anything. It was one of the situations where you reacted before anything ever really happened. Don't know what I'm talking about? I guess that only happens to me.

"Oh gosh, did I run over your foot by accident?" I looked up and see that Sheriff Deputy Ethan Bradley was on the other end of the piano trying to roll it down the hallway of the apartment building.

"No, sorry. Knee jerk reaction." He grinned at me and I'm sure he thought I was a bit on the weird side, but oh well. I had spoken to Deputy Bradley a few times whenever he came into The Diner to get breakfast along with Sheriff Hennings. He was pleasant and he was a total looker if you were into the whole cowboy persona, but really in the end he didn't give me butterflies. Not like Mike did.

"What are you doing with this piano Deputy Bradley?"

"Now please, it's Ethan."

"Ok, Ethan," I gave him an added smile.

"My great aunt lived here and just passed away. I was going to take this down the service elevator and then after that I haven't a clue." He stood to his full height which was impressive, he had to be almost six foot four. And he had the broadest shoulders that I had ever seen, he would've made an amazing football player with just his stature and size. He wasn't what I would call chunky, the word I would use to describe

Deputy Bradley would be solid. Like a freaking rock.

I placed a hand on my chest to show my sympathy, "I'm so sorry to hear that Dep-I mean Ethan."

"Really, it's alright. It was her time, she had lived a full and eventful life. She often taught piano lessons around here so she has this piano leftover. The manager of the apartment said that I could leave it downstairs for now until I found a home for it."

I touched my fingers the top of the wood of the upright piano and walked my way around the front, trailing my hand against the grain. I lifted the fall, which housed the keys, and unveiled the glorious black and white pieces of heaven. It had been so long since I've played on anything other than my keyboard that my hands were itching to just touch the keys if even for a moment.

I reached down and then snapped my hand back, looking up at Ethan, "May I?"

"Have at it." He said without the least bit of uncertainty.

I touched my hands to the keys and just let instinct takeover. I began the intro to "Moonlight Sonata" by Beethoven, which was my favorite go to piece. This piece was remarkably simple and was mostly comprised of repetitive hand movements, but I just loved its sound.

One thing about me since piano used to be my entire life, I really got into my piece whenever I was playing it. Accomplishing this standing up was a task, but menial.

A minute or so had passed and I opened my eyes and realized that I had totally gotten lost in the sound of the music and quickly removed my hands from off of the keys.

"I'm sorry, I didn't mean to get so into it."

"Don't be sorry. If I had half of the passion that you do for the piano, maybe I would've stuck with it. Aunt Edna hated trying to teach me piano." He cocked a brow as if he were deep in thought, "I have an idea. Why don't you keep the piano? I really don't know what to do with it, no one in my family wants it. And I can tell that you are devoted to the instrument."

I replaced the fall, protecting the keys once again before I looked back up into Ethan's eyes. "It used to be my whole life. But are you sure? This was such a big important part of your aunt's life."

"Sheridan, I couldn't be more certain. My aunt would've wanted her beloved piano to go to someone who would care for it and treasure it the way she had."

I released a smile that reached all the way up to my eyes and I just felt elated. I knew that there would've been no way to bring my baby grand piano here without it costing a fortune to haul it professionally, so having an upright piano was the next best thing.

I hurriedly unlocked the door to my apartment and found the perfect spot for it right against the entry wall. I had to move an entryway table out of the way to make room for it, but once it was in position, it looked like it was made to be there.

I finally had to pry myself away from work and my apartment, so Grady let me into Emmy Lou's so I could check out his piano to see if it needed tuning or not. All I had to end up doing was adjusting the tension of a few of the piano strings and it would be in tip top condition. I also took the time to dust and clean the finish since it looked like it had been forgotten in the corner of the room for quite some time now.

Using a dampened cloth, I was making sure that every little piece of the piano was cleaned to my satisfaction. It may not get used much around here but at least I would be happy with the final product.

I heard some hushed whispers from out on the stage. I was

in the backroom which was just off to the back of the stage, so it was really easy to overhear.

"Brock where the hell has Mike been? I called for a mandatory practice and here he didn't show." That voice sounded a lot like Toby.

"He just got back from St. Louis, he went to visit his dad. Apparently some bad shit went down between him and Sheridan." At the mere mention of my name, I perked up a bit and began leaning my way towards the door so I could hear just a bit clearer. I was leaning so far off the piano bench that I was really surprised that I didn't go toppling to the floor especially after what was said next.

"Sheridan hasn't mentioned anything to me about it," Toby almost sounded as if he were a little hurt that I didn't come running to him about my problems. He had no idea what he would've been asking for.

"I don't know, but when Mike called me to look after Sadie he sounded pissed and he sounded hurt. He has never been one to spill about his feelings, but I could tell that he was really into her. Something bad enough happened to where he kicked her out of his house."

"So that was why she was all gung ho about moving into Maggie's apartment. I really wonder if Sheridan will stick around here now since things fell apart with them."

I had just about enough of hearing them talk about me behind my back. Why wouldn't I stay here just because Mike and I weren't friends anymore or whatever the hell we were?

Now was a perfect time as any to make sure the piano was completely tuned, so I began playing so I could *tune* out the gossiping going on out on the stage.

And they said women gossip, sheesh.

I started playing the first song that came to mind. I would on any given day openly admit my love for this woman, to accomplish as much as she has during her lifetime and career is an amazing feat. So I began playing "You Haven't Seen The Last Of Me," sung by Cher in the movie *Burlesque*. Her voice was my guilty pleasure and I remembered singing to more than one of her songs into my hairbrush while looking into my mirror growing up.

This song was mostly played on the piano with accompanying drums but all I needed was my hands and the eighty-eight keys underneath them.

She sang of not ever giving up on her hopes and dreams. And it pertained to me as well.

They didn't know me enough to gossip about me behind my back, good or otherwise. I've been brought to the end of my rope before and I thought I was doing pretty well for myself now considering the circumstances. Granted things would be complete if I had Benjamin with me and yes, also if I had Mike back in my life once again.

I was so into playing that I didn't realize that I had begun to sing as well. I haven't sang in front of anyone or even in public in several years and I had vowed never to do so again. I knew that I wasn't even close to being up on the same stratosphere as Cher in singing, but I thought I was pretty decent. Pate squashed those dreams when he broke my hands. He told me that I would've never amounted to anything as a singer or a pianist and that I sucked and it was better this way.

You didn't want that type of negativity to sink in but since I heard it so often, I ultimately started to believe him.

I would often be humming or singing to myself while cleaning up the kitchen or cooking dinner because what else did I have to do? He would come up behind me and smack me on the back of my head telling me that I sounded awful and to shut up. So I just stopped singing. I don't know why I didn't ever stop wanting to play piano, but the not wanting to sing in front of people always stuck with me.

I finished the song and just sat there staring at the keys

with my hands placed in my lap. I didn't know that I had an audience until I heard several sets of claps behind me. I gasped and swung around on the bench to see Brock, Toby, and Grady standing there with their mouths almost literally hanging open, slapping their open palms together.

My cheeks became inflamed as I felt the blush creep its way up my body.

"I...I'm sorry. I didn't mean to start singing, I know you are just being nice."

"Doll face, I am nothing if not honest. And that was one heck of a performance." Toby boasted, and he hung a hand out, "Now, I know my Cher and girl you just brought it up a notch," he finished with a snap which caused me to chuckle.

I supposed that I could forget about their gossip fest.

I looked down at my hands and just shrugged my shoulders, "Thank you," I replied ever so softly.

"Hey, I have an idea. The Nation's Capital is performing Friday night, how about you come on before them and just perform one song?" Grady chimed in with his brilliant to him plan.

I didn't know how to respond, before this would've been a dream come true performing a song in front of an audience for their listening pleasure. But I've been out of the spotlight so long I didn't know if I would be able to calm my nerves enough to go on.

I made a last minute spontaneous decision, "I would love to perform a piece on the piano, but I don't know if I can sing along with it. It's been a long time since I've sang in front of an audience and I stopped doing so because of one person's remarks to me. I just don't want you to be disappointed if I just end up playing an instrumental piece."

"Hey, don't worry about it. Just the small piece you played a few minutes ago blew me away, I could only imagine what an intricate piece would do." Grady added.

Brock finally chimed in, "Whoever said anything bad to you regarding your singing abilities was a fucking dumbass. You need to know that what we three just heard was brilliant." He sheepishly placed his hand in his pocket and turned and walked out of the room. I knew he would be on Mike's side once he found out everything that went on between the two of us, but it was nice to get that reaffirmation from him.

CHAPTER 19

Mike

It had only been a few days, but things were just too lonely at home. Sadie was either whimpering or pouting and didn't even want to play fetch with her favorite yellow tennis ball. I knew we both felt the same, I just didn't know what to do about it.

I heard what my father had to say, but I still haven't come to terms on what to do just yet. Brock told me that he ran into Sheridan just the other day so I knew she was still in Brown County, which lessened the brick that was laying on my chest just a little.

Bringing my favorite coffee mug to my mouth, I took a generous sip. It's still rather hot, but it just tasted bland. Sheridan made the best coffee, it never had a tasteless flavor whenever she made it. *It's because she made it with love.*

Releasing a deep sigh, I poured the remainder of my colored water down the drain in my kitchen sink and watched the liquid swirl around the stainless steel basin until it settled down the siphon.

An idea sprouted in my head and I hoped like hell it was

going to work. I had to be at work here in a bit, but on my downtime when I didn't have a run, I would stop by the diner and get a cup of coffee from there.

Yeah, that would be my exact reason in going to the diner, I needed flavor in my life because this unsavory crap wasn't going to cut it anymore.

And if I just so happened to run into Sheridan hopefully some spark of a plan would come to mind on what to do.

That was my mantra that I was sticking to, I was *not* going to the diner just to see Sheridan. I just needed a decent cup of coffee. Sounded brilliant and believable to me.

Sitting in the passenger seat of the ambulance, my partner Todd pulled into the concrete parking lot of The Diner and parked in an empty parking space at the edge of the lot.

It had been one hell of a day and now I really was in need of that cup of coffee.

The sun was setting and the gentle glowing of rich amber colors were fading into the horizon. Another day was almost complete. Another day without my Sheridan.

It was almost funny referring to her as mine because I really didn't have the right to label her as such. She was never ever mine to begin with, so the point was completely moot. Wishful thinking I suppose.

Todd was the first to exit the ambulance, he was a middle-aged man with salt and pepper hair, becoming more and more salt colored as he continued to work with me. I quickly followed suit, exiting the ambulance and making sure the doors were locked.

We had several runs today luckily nothing being life threatening, which made it all in all a good day, even if we did have to run our asses off. We even had to sign off midway through our shift to restock the bus of things that we had run out of.

Walking behind Todd, I saw the illuminating red neon lights that the outside of The Diner was decorated in, they must have just came on with dusk approaching. You definitely wouldn't ever be able to miss this place at night. He entered through the front door first and I took my time looking around the establishment to see if anyone I knew was in attendance. I wouldn't outright admit that I was only really looking for Sheridan. Even if I was, I didn't see her standing at any of the tables.

"Hey, Deputy Bradley," I heard Todd say to Ethan, but I couldn't see because he was in my direct line of sight. He inched towards the man, which opened up my view on... Sheridan. But it was what she was doing that had me intrigued presently.

She currently had her open hand covering the top of Ethan Bradley's. I had to do a double to take to really lock in that what I was seeing wasn't just a figment of my imagination. And indeed seeing their elusive handholding a second time just twisted that knife that already pierced my heart just a bit further.

Rage boiled deep in my gut and it was almost too much to handle, I felt as if I were a volcano on the crest of erupting. She was now seeing fucking Ethan Bradley? Wow, the connection that I thought I imagined must have been just that, but that didn't mean that it hurt any less.

"Mike!" Todd snapped his fingers in front of my face startling me out of my delusion.

"Yah," I bit out realizing that I was still looking at their connected hands. I looked up at Todd with my brows furrowed and my nostrils flared. Just then, I turned my line of vision up to meet Sheridan's wide eyes, the penitence on her face was remarkable, like she was caught doing something that she wasn't supposed to.

I didn't know why she would've felt that way, we weren't anything, right?

"I suddenly don't want any coffee from *her.*"

"Her?" Ethan said straightening up his posture from where he was leaning on the counter with a menacing look taking root on his face.

"*Here*…I said here." I didn't of course, but who was he to argue to me about something he knew absolutely nothing about. But then again if Sheridan was fucking Bradley, perhaps he knew more than I did about her because, at this time, I felt as if knew absolutely nothing.

I pivoted my work boot on the floor turning in the opposite direction from my audience and shoved open the glass door that was outlined in metal, making it come close to hitting the aluminum siding. I needed to calm myself down because that was all I needed to end up having to pay for a broken door.

I took a few deep breaths filling my lungs with the fresh air from outside. Deep inhalation in and letting it slowly release out through my nose.

"What the hell was that?" Todd said as he came out from The Diner finding me seated on the back bumper of the ambulance my navy work pant clad legs were crossed at the ankle and stretched out in front of me. He was carrying his cup of coffee and I regretted openly denying myself a cup. I missed Sheridan's coffee, but more importantly I missed her.

Apparently she didn't reciprocate those feelings which made me feel like a failure all over again. I believed that it was safe to say that I was a failure at keeping anyone in my life.

I deserved my life of solitude, I just didn't want it.

"Jameson what the hell, man?" He jerked his boot up kicking my crossed feet apart further trying to get my attention.

I unfolded my arms and pushed myself off of the bus and walked around to the passenger side door banging my open palm on the back of the bus on my way, which signified that I was ready to go.

I couldn't trust myself to speak. I was never really one to open up about my feelings and Sheridan had been the first in an extremely long time. Things were better off when I was closed off and a recluse.

I still had several hours left on my shift, in one instance I was hoping for radio silence, but the other I wanted to keep busy so my mind didn't wander back to things that couldn't ever possibly be.

One thing I knew was that I had to call Brock. I took my phone out of the cell holster that was attached to my belt, whenever I was on shift it was much easier to grab my phone from off of the side of my hip instead of digging around in my pocket. I found Brock's name and pressed send and waited for him to answer.

"Hey, Mike," he greeted happily on the other end of the line.

"Hey, uh, do me a favor, will ya? Change the brakes on Sheridan's car and then call her to let her know that it's ready. I won't have time to work on it anytime soon and she needs a car." That was a blatant lie, I had time to work on it, I just couldn't bear to actually do it anymore. The truth was that it could've been done ages ago, but it was my way of keeping Sheridan around.

I guess that didn't make me any better than Pate. Sure, I didn't *force* her to stay but I wasn't exactly relishing on her freedom.

"Sure, thing man! Oh and don't forget that we are playing at Emmy Lou's tomorrow night." I rolled my eyes consciously knowing that he wouldn't be able to see my reaction. I had no desire to play tomorrow night, but I had a duty to the band and I wouldn't leave them hanging.

"Alright, what time should I make myself known?"

"Be there at six-thirty so we can get everything set up. And be sure to wear a smile, even if it is just a forced one. I don't really know what's going on, but you are retreating back to your former pathetic self."

"Got it," I replied in my most enthusiastic tone before I ended the call on him. I threw my phone down in my lap and laid my head back on the headrest only moments before we got a call to head to the local nursing home.

Flipping on the lights and turning on the siren, we were on our way to do what we were trained to do; save lives. It didn't help that, in the furthest back recesses of my mind, I wished that things would've turned out differently for the one who saved mine.

Rushing my way into the front door of the bar, I looked down at my watch to see it was six-thirty on the nose. I was extremely lucky to make it on time. After getting off of shift at seven am this morning, I tossed and turned in my bed until I finally fell asleep around noon. Which meant that I overslept my alarm and luckily was awoken by a whimpering Sadie who wanted to go outside.

Work was hellacious after leaving The Diner. The call we received from dispatch to the nursing home ended up being a case where we had to wait for the coroner. It never got any easier seeing someone die. It was a part of my job that I didn't enjoy, especially when it happened on my watch it always hit a little too close to home.

A beer was definitely calling my name so I made a b-line to the bar before I even went to seek out the other members of the band. But it seemed as if they were on the same wave length as me as they were all sitting at the bar having a drink. Now this wasn't an uncommon occurrence but it was odd for them to be altogether before a set.

Normally Toby was running around like a chicken with his head cut off making sure that his choice of outfit for the night was up to par. Brock almost always was in the backroom making sure his guitar was in tip top working order for the night. Charlie was another one of the easy going guys in the group, he was often late and showed up right before it was time to be on stage. So the fact that he was here, on time was weird in and of itself, especially since he and Maggie were back together.

I seriously felt as if I was in the middle of the twilight zone has they all three simultaneously turned around on their bar stools to where they were now facing the stage. I caught Grady out of the corner of my eye and lifted my hand in the air signaling that I wanted a beer. There was only one kind that I drank and he knew that was all I ever got while being here.

Tessa was the one to bring me back my beer also bringing her husband, Brock a refill as well. But instead of leaving, she put her elbows down on the countertop and leaned into her hands.

"I am so excited, I cannot wait," she said. I had no absolute clue what she was talking about so I didn't hesitate in asking.

"Oh, it's just the newest Brown County Babe is performing tonight before y'all go onstage."

"Tell me Tessa, what is the Brown County Babes and who do they entail?" I hadn't a clue what she was referring to as I had never heard that term before. It was endearing I supposed calling a group of her friends the Brown County Babes. Or maybe it was a new all girl group in the area, that would be a great variety.

Cupping her hand to her ear pretending that someone was yelling for her, "What's that Grady?" Trying to turn in the opposite direction she was desperately tried waving me off but I reached over the counter and caught her by the elbow, she wasn't getting out of this so easily.

"It's nothing big, Toby just dubbed a few of us girls as Brown County Babes. There is of course me, Emmalynne, Maggie, and now…" She trailed off on the latest newcomer and once I heard the sound coming from the piano she didn't need to fill in the blanks, I could handle that task just fine.

I took a more than generous swig from my green tinted beer bottle before I turned to give the guys the most menacing look that I could muster up.

I didn't know if I could actually turn around and look at her.

She seemed to be doing a quick warm up exercise that had the entire audience into it when I glanced all around me, but still not being able to turn in her direction.

Then she actually started speaking into the microphone, introducing herself.

"Ahem… Good evening, everyone. You'll have to excuse my nervousness it's been," she quickly took a deep breath, and I could hear her releasing it into the microphone, "quite a long time since I've performed for a crowd. My intention is to sing, but with my nerves I'm not sure if it'll be a possibility." I couldn't believe what I was hearing, she was actually going to sing.

I polished off my beer before I finally made the brave decision to turn around and as soon as my eyes connected with hers my breath whooshed out of my body. She looked exquisite. Her hair hung down her back in curly ringlets and the way the piano was set up on the stage I could tell that she was wearing a light teal dress with a cream sweater over it. The dress hit her mid-thigh while she was sitting down on the piano bench. I could see fragments of her bare feet on the pedals that were connected to the bottom of the piano.

It almost made me crack a small grin to know that she couldn't wear shoes while playing.

And of course to strike me dead right here where I was standing, she was wearing her signature ruby red lipstick. I didn't know anyone else who could make that color look so goddamn enticing.

I could just imagine her succulent red lips wrapped around my straining cock, staining it crimson as she took it deep within the alcove of her mouth. Only that could never happen now since she was with Ethan. And that did absolutely nothing for my overbearing erection.

You could see the presence of her nerves as she began speaking again. Her hands were faintly shaking as she adjusted the microphone that was on a stand in front of her, making it to where it was a little more easily accessible. "So if you would, please just bear with me, I would greatly appreciate it." She finally broke her eye contact with me as she went on. "This song really hits home for me. I never intended on ever coming to Brown County, but someone thought it was crucial in my making an appearance. And although there are hundreds and possibly thousands of different ways that it could've happened, a certain person took a risk by driving impaired and collided with my car." She began shaking her head back and forth, "No this isn't a public service announcement about drinking and driving, although I could very well turn it into one. After all, I do have the mic." She giggled and then winked at someone in the crowd. She was working them and they were eating out of the palm of her hand.

You could tell that she was relaxing because her posture wasn't as pronounced and the shaking in her hands had ceased. She was becoming comfortable with everyone. I was on the verge of praying that she would sing because I wanted to finally get to hear her beautiful melodic singing voice. If it was anything like the woman before me, it would absolutely astound me.

"And as much as I want to be furious with that person, in the end I would've never taken a chance on Brown County and then ultimately made it my home. There was one special person who went above and beyond their duty, especially with us being perpetual strangers, and helped me out with no questions asked. We became friends and I always had the hopes to become something more, but that wasn't meant to be because I held a very huge part of me back from him. I just hope that one day he can forgive me for doing what I felt needed to be done." She took a hand and wiped her cheek, no doubt trying to erase any sign of tears falling from her eyes.

Forgiveness… That was funny because that was one thing that I was trying to do. Maybe it would've been easier for me to accept things if she wouldn't have been so quick to jump into the arms of another.

"I would also like to introduce someone you already know, Emmalynne Morgan. I've heard through some pretty justifiable sources, mainly being her fiancé Grady that she is the woman behind the name of Emmy Lou's. I think that is incredibly romantic. But anyways, I'm getting off topic here," waving out a hand, "she has graciously accepted to help me out tonight by playing the drums."

Emmy walked out onto the stage with her set of drum sticks and everyone clapped. She was like the sweetheart of Brown County. Emmalynne made the most incredible desserts and was the owner of Turn the Page Bookstore. She did a little curtsey and sat behind a drum kit. My drum kit. I was so preoccupied with Sheridan's presence on the stage that I failed to realize that my drum kit was the only other instrument set up on the stage beside the piano.

My focus was strictly back to Sheridan. If I had been sitting down, I would've been on the edge of my seat with anticipation.

I had hoped that Sheridan would stick around until after our set then maybe I could get her alone to talk. I didn't see Ethan around, so maybe that was a possibility.

Sheridan adjusted her seating once again and placed her hands on top of the piano keys as she closed her eyes. Seconds ticked by and just when people were starting to look at each other with confused expressions she opened her eyes and began the song.

After the first few notes were released from her fingertips and her mouth connected with the microphone beginning to lightly sing the beginning words, I knew exactly what song she was playing. Then Emmalynne came in on the beat.

"How To Save A Life" by The Fray was what was coming out of those delicious red lips. Lips that reminded me of blood, singing a song that reminded me of losing Hannah. I couldn't look away from how into the song Sheridan was getting, I was drawn to her like a moth to a flame. Her sultry voice was so mesmerizing and it was a true shame that she decided against going to Juilliard to perform. A lot of people were missing out on this amazing spectacle that was Sheridan.

The song was a sensual message she was sending to me. Together we did save each other's life. Something that might not have ever happened had we not met. She was right in saying that someone desperately wanted her to be here in Brown County at the exact moment that she was. If it wasn't for that dickhead who made the decision to drive drunk, I might never have been introduced to the woman who owned my heart.

I felt as if I were Robert Frost, meandering down that path when I come upon that fork in the road. On one hand, I could fight for Sheridan, make her realize that we belonged together. And as much as it may hurt sometimes not having Hannah around, become a father again. On the other hand, I could become a recluse once again, not trusting anyone in and keeping everything to myself, which would only cause me to combust at one point or another.

Did I stand up to the plate and be a true man to become the one thing I said I never wanted again to be with the woman I was supposed to be with?

By the time she played and sang the very last note, I knew exactly what I was going to do. It was just putting it into action.

She stood from her position on the piano bench and ran a hand down her dress, smoothing out the wrinkles as she came to stand in front of the piano. She broke out in the biggest and brightest smile I had ever seen and did a simple little curtsy as the entire audience and myself broke out into a massive standing ovation. She placed both hands over her heart, she looked as if she was truly proud of herself as she should be. She accomplished something simply amazing here tonight.

A hand came up and grabbed my shoulder, giving it a firm squeeze. I looked over my shoulder to see that Brock had sided up next to me. "She was amazing, huh?"

"That she was, man." I wanted to sing her praises. I wanted to go and sweep her into my arms. But those fantasy thoughts came crashing down in a screeching halt as her smile became even brighter when she jumped off of the stage and into Ethan Bradley's awaiting arms.

My jaw hardened as I began gritting my teeth. I caught Brock looking at me from my peripheral vision as he then turned to see what had caught my attention. I knew the moment he realized what was happening because he shoved me towards the stage where Charlie and Toby had already started setting up.

He knew that I was about to erupt, so he kept ahold of my collar until I jerked out of his grasp. I continued to storm towards the stage but only being able to see red. There was that fucking color again.

Red the color of love, lust, blood, and broken hearts.

So many different shitty things were associated with the color and here I was drawn to it like a magnet. I set myself up for this, for all of it.

I stomped my boots up the stairs and yanked my drum sticks out of Toby's hand when he offered them to me as I went by.

I took my place behind my drum kit and I knew that it was going to get the brunt of my anger tonight. I just hoped that it would withhold the brutality.

Toby, for once, didn't give an entire spiel before he wanted to start the show. That was very unlike Toby, but he had been quite a bit moodier since Maggie's earlier kidnapping. Don't ask, don't tell was my motto from here on out. I didn't want to know about anything 'happy' or 'sad' going on in anyone's lives and it would be best for them to pay me the same respects.

Toby grabbed ahold of the microphone stand and then pivoted his foot to where he was looking at each of us, "'Mr. Brightside' first, yeah?"

I immediately shook my head no. That was *not* the song that I wanted to begin our show with, especially with the events that were unfolding right before me.

The other two members agreed with Toby to start off with that, so I was outvoted. The Killers for the win.

Charlie started us out on the bass intro and I took my cue from him tapping on the snare.

I began slamming down the sticks on my drums as the song went on. I didn't want to look, but I couldn't take my eyes off the scene in front of me, it was like a fucking car wreck, drawing in my attention to see what would happen next. It was as if the song was playing out right in front of me.

They were looking into each other's eyes as she placed her open hand on his chest almost in a loving way. What really took the cake was when she reached up on her tiptoes and kissed his cheek, then a faint hue dusted her cheeks as she blushed.

So this was what jealousy felt like. The envy was ripping me apart from the inside. And I'll have to admit I didn't like it one bit.

Jealousy wasn't something I was used to and it would be a hard thing for me to admit, but I was so fucking jealous. Those were my kisses and that hand was made to caress *me.*

At this point, I wished that I had never met her again. To think that I almost admitted to her that I loved her and would do anything to be with her, even if it meant opening up my heart for another child.

I could just see them going back to his place and him stripping her free from her dress. I have never pounded on my drums so hard before, but they were taking a fucking beating. A beating that I imagined that I was giving to Ethan Bradley. Ethan fucking Bradley…

Continuing my assault, at the very last moment before the song was over with Sheridan's eyes connected with mine once again. After the last beat, I threw down my drumsticks and stood up, knocking down my stool with the sheer force of my movements.

I was sure I looked completely sinister and threatening as I stalked towards them, my eyes hardened in a stare and my veins in my neck bulging out. I wasn't able to control my anger any longer and things were about to get ugly.

A look of fear crossed Sheridan's face as I continued my way towards them, which made me lose some of my luster. I didn't want to scare her, that was never my intention and I sure as hell didn't like seeing that look being put on her face by me. So I changed my plans once again, walking straight through the two of them and veered towards the exit.

Once I got back home I didn't stop to say hello to Sadie, I just went directly to my room and plummeted on my bed. I wanted to cry, I wanted to scream so loudly to get out all of my frustrations. Damn Sheridan for making me fall in love with her.

She was supposed to be the one to save me. My own personal hell was pulling me down into the deep abyss again and she was supposed to be the one to save me.

I repeatedly pounded my fists into my pillow, throwing out every single obscenity I could until it made me feel better. There was really no telling how long this went on but when I finally caught something out of the corner of my eye it made me stop dead in my tracks.

I threw my legs over the side of my bed and rested my chin in my hands as I stared at the objects that dared to mock me.

Perched upon my dresser was the brand new St. Louis ball cap that Sheridan bought for me with her first paycheck. She had been so excited to buy me something, then I had to go and crush her hopes by telling her the backstory behind the meaning of my tattered hat. I shoved off of my bed and walked two steps forward until I reached my dresser. I lifted up the neon yellow post-it that contained the word 'Thanks,' written by Sheridan's hand when she left my house.

I couldn't bear to get rid of the baseball cap, but that didn't stop me from crumpling the written thank you in the palm of my hand.

My chest felt as if someone placed a cinder block on top of it and I wanted so badly to take a sledgehammer and bust it to smithereens. I didn't like feeling this way. And with the impact that Sheridan had on me, I didn't feel as if this sensation was going to go away anytime soon.

CHAPTER 20

Sheridan

I had done it. I couldn't believe that I dug deep down and banded together all of my courage and actually performed in front of a bar full of people. It was such a euphoric feeling and all I wanted to do was rush to Mike and hear him tell me how proud of me he was.

But I had come here with Ethan and it was his arms that were outstretched and waiting for me when I rushed offstage.

I couldn't be rude and just brush Ethan off completely, he had been a major help to me these past few days. He and I had been spending quite a bit of time together after he gave me his great aunt's piano. Between grieving the loss of his great Aunt Edna and then a few days later the breakup between him and his boyfriend, he really needed a shoulder to lean on. And I had two available shoulders and I was great at listening, so I was ready to be there for him when he needed me.

Ethan had just told me about his breakup with Owen when Mike walked into the diner the other night with his partner, Todd. I was sympathetic towards Ethan since almost the same thing had just happened to me. Mike and I weren't technically together, but that didn't mean I didn't feel the effects of a broken heart. My love for Mike had snuck up on me, but I truly and deeply was in love with Mike Jameson. And the look that crossed his face when he saw my hand covering Ethan's in a caring gesture was one that I quickly wanted to forget. But just saw once again mere moments earlier as he stormed between Ethan and me on his way retreating out the door.

I never knew Mike to be one to jump to conclusions, but tonight was now the third time he has done so. If he had just stopped and heard me out, many things and ill feelings could've very well been avoided.

Ethan had paid me enormous compliments and I wanted to thank him, so I kissed his cheek showing my appreciation. I knew Mike had seen the little exchange because the beating on his drum accelerated tenfold.

You could see the anger radiating off of him in waves. And truthfully he freaked me out a bit. I never knew him to want to go all He-Man on someone. Ethan was much larger than Mike and even though he was the Sheriff Deputy of Brown County, I still think he was quaking in his cowboy boots.

"What the hell was that all about?" Ethan asked with a quizzical look on his face and I could tell that he was getting ready to go into Deputy mode.

He turned to take off after Mike and I gently caught him by the arm. "Just let him go, Ethan. It isn't you, it's because of me. I've done something to hurt him and now he's showing signs of jealousy obviously because I am here with you. But true to typical Mike he's jumping the gun without knowing what's going on. But really I can't blame him because I kept something big from him."

"It's the reason you and him aren't together now, right? It couldn't have been that bad."

I contemplated telling him all about Pate and Benjamin. I mean in the end it could only help that a law enforcement official knew about it, right?

"Let's go outside. I think there are some things that you should know."

I made it to the parking lot with Ethan hot on my heels, pulling my cream cardigan around my waist and crossing my arms in front of my chest. Being that it was still summer it was abnormal for such a chill to be in the air, especially with it being Georgia.

I walked a little further around the fully packed parking lot kicking rocks with my flats as I moved around. Ethan stuffed his hands into his pockets of his Levi jeans. He looked extremely country tonight with his cowboy boots, tight Levi's and his plaid button down shirt tucked into his jeans. The only thing that would polish off his look would be a belt buckle and a cowboy hat. I leaned forward to check and low and behold he actually did have a belt buckle. I had to chuckle.

"Ok, hold on." I stopped walking and stood in front of Ethan, pointing to his buckle. "What does that say?" I couldn't really tell because of the lighting in the parking lot, the entire lot was only illuminated by two single street lamps.

He turned it to where it would shine in the light and on the pewter belt buckle was 'World's Largest Nuts' with a nut and bolt on either side of the writing. I looked up at him with a cocked brow, "Really? Really Ethan?"

He lifted one side of his mouth in a small and innocent grin then shrugged his shoulders.

"Whatever," I rolled my eyes and then continued on walking around the lot.

"So, I guess there is really no good place to start so I'll just dive into it. I won't go into Mike's personal life because it isn't my place to say, but I will say that I never told him that I had a son. He found out whenever he took me home to see my dad in the hospital after he had a heart attack. "

I went on to tell him about Pate Strickland and he listened intently. It felt good to get absolutely everything out in the open and with Ethan knowing he could help be on the lookout for Pate.

It was nice not having to check over my shoulder every five minutes. I had been in Brown County for several months now and he hadn't come around. It felt exhilarating to finally be free.

I couldn't be happier, I had my son with me in my home. But even still, my heart wasn't completely whole. A piece was missing in the form of a tall man with brown hair and piercing hazel eyes. I missed Mike. I missed my best friend.

"Now you be good for Tessa, alright?" I told Ben as I was crouched down in front of him in The Morgan's living room. I adjusted his glasses because they never really seemed to keep straight on his little face. Boys and all of their rough housing, I would never understand.

"I will, mommy," he replied with a whisper cautiously looking in Tessa's direction. I had to brace myself for the possibility of the onslaught of tears to begin streaming down his face since I was leaving him. He was still getting used to being in a new place and actually being able to be with me all the time.

I enveloped Ben in a hug and he squeezed me tightly before letting go and giving me an Eskimo kiss.

I stood from my place on the floor and watched my little man run off to play with Blake Morgan. Dodged the tears bullet today. Tessa and her mother in law had been a godsend, one of them always offered to watch Benjamin while I was at work. I told them that, at any time, I could find a more permanent sitter, but they wouldn't hear of it, Tessa actually told me not to be 'redonkulous' perhaps one of these days I would get used to her outrageous lingo. When Tessa was working her mother in law watched Blake so they said it was nice to have another little boy around the same age for him to play with.

It was a huge relief to have someone that I knew and trusted watch my son.

Ben had been here for just a few weeks and together we had adjusted pretty well. Wanda knew that I wouldn't work much overtime now since my son was with me, so we've gotten our schedules fixed to what would work out well for us both. She even hired a part-time waitress to work at night so I was able to leave at a decent time.

I couldn't deny the lonely feeling that I felt at night whenever I would lie in my bed thinking of Mike, hoping he was just in the room next to me, or my ultimate dream, actually lying right next to me.

I left The Morgan's and got in my new to me car, and went on about my way to work. I wished that I could say that I was surprised to be hearing from Brock when he called about my car but that would've been a lie. Mike had basically cut all ties from me and I really couldn't blame him. Everything just led up to a downward spiral, first with me not telling him about Ben, then him jumping to his own conclusions about Ethan. Ethan didn't openly advertise himself as being gay, but he didn't hide it either. His business was his own and I wasn't about to openly seek out Mike just to tell him that Ethan wasn't into me nor was I into him. He had made his decision and as much as that hurt, I had to move on with my life because of my son.

I made it into work a few minutes before my shift started and I didn't hesitate to tie my apron around my waist and set out making fresh coffee.

Today was an unusually slow day for The Diner so I made sure to keep myself busy by making sure all of the counters and tables were continuously wiped clean and all of the condiments and metal napkin dispensers were filled.

Wanda had just stepped through the door to the kitchen to go outback to take her break and I was finishing up with a customer.

Tipping up the coffee pot making sure that I got the last of the hot brown liquid into the cup placed on the table in front of my customer, I smiled to them and said, "Please let me know if you need anything else."

I turned around and directly into a brick wall of a chest as a hand wrapped around my upper arm, digging into my flesh.

Slowly tipping my head to where I could look into the eyes of the owner of this body, I couldn't believe the set of ice cold eyes staring back at me.

I took two steps back trying to get away from the person when I felt the handle to the coffee pot slip from my grasp and quickly fall to the floor, breaking into hundreds of tiny little pieces.

"P…Pate," I barely got out through my trembling voice.

"Tsk. Tsk. Sheridan," he leaned towards my ear and said. Having his hot breath on my skin made me tremble in fear.

This wasn't happening.

This couldn't be happening.

He continued on, "I'm going to give you five minutes to get this mess cleaned up and out into my car willfully before I come back in and drag you out myself, making a scene. And if you don't come out on your own, there will be consequences for little Ben." My eyes bulged out of my head and my legs felt as if they were going to crumble.

How did he know about Ben?

He placed his hands on my cheeks and directed my face up to where I was forced to look in his eyes. "Do I make myself clear?"

"Yes, sir," I said instantly thrown back into being that scared woman who felt inadequate and insecure.

He let go of my arm and left as quickly as he came

leaving me a terrified shaking mess.

I could feel the walls begin to force in on me, but I couldn't let them, I didn't have time. I couldn't let anything happen to Ben.

I turned towards the kitchen to see Archie looking at me through the serving window.

I glanced down towards my feet at the broken shards of glass, "The coffee pot slipped out of my hands. I'll get the broom." Lowering my head, I went to retrieve the broom and dustpan to dispose of my mess. Luckily this wasn't the first time so hopefully no one would be none the wiser.

I had to quickly think about what to do because I didn't have much time remaining. The thing about Pate was when he said he was going to do something, he would do it. So I had no doubt in my mind that he would come back into The Diner and drag me out kicking and screaming. He had never done anything forcefully to me in public, but he's had several months to stew on my leaving. And here to think that I thought that I was completely safe and now out of harm's way. But now I had to protect Ben. No one would come between my son and me anymore.

I went behind the counter retrieving my purse and walked through the swinging door that led towards the kitchen. Archie had his back to me busy making food and cleaning the grill so he had no idea that I was picking out a knife from the butcher block and slipping it into my purse.

If things came down to it, I wouldn't hesitate to take matters into my own hands.

"Uh Archie. Something came up and I'm going to have to leave. I'm sorry for it being such short notice."

He had stopped what he was doing and turned around to face me. Giving me a stern look, "Are you sure everything is ok?" Archie was more like a second father to me rather than a boss. He had that protective instinct.

I tried to let out a lighthearted giggle, but I was pretty sure that I failed, "Everything is fine. Nothing to worry about."

"Well alright, call and let us know if you need anything." The vibe he was giving off led me to think that he didn't believe my lie. Even though I had never been any good at lying, I didn't know what else to do.

I knew my time was quickly running out so I rushed through the glass and metal front door to the diner making sure to keep my purse close to me at all times.

True to his word, Pate was standing in the concrete parking lot, casually leaning against his car as if he wasn't about to commit a crime.

Apparently I wasn't walking fast enough for him so he stormed over to me and grabbed my arm once again as I tried to cower away from him.

"I wouldn't do that if I were you, Sheridan."

He opened the back driver's side door before he wretched my purse out of my grasp and threw it on the other side of the car. Then he proceeded to yank my arms behind my back and secure my hands together. Feeling the hard plastic bite into my skin, I knew his handcuff of choice was a zip tie.

My brain was working overtime trying to think of various ways to escape.

Pushing down on the top of my head to get me to crouch down, he placed a hand on my upper back and shoved me into the backseat in the same manner as my purse. That's all I was to him, an object to do with as he saw fit.

Looking back through the window, I saw his smooth the wrinkles out of his suit jacket and unbutton the one button that held it together in front of his stomach so he could move a little more freely. Then he glanced around and all I could do was hope that someone saw the assault that just occurred.

Pate opened the driver's side door and smoothly slid behind the wheel to his luxurious car and cranked the engine.

He wasted no time leaving the parking lot and going in the direction of wherever he was taking me.

I was laying on my side, which wasn't comfortable at all and there was no possible way for me to move to be able to sit up and see where we were going. I hoped to God that he wasn't going to take me back to his house out of Brown County.

It didn't take him long before I saw him adjust the rearview mirror to where he could see my face and I could see his.

"Do you honestly think that I'm stupid, Sheridan? I saw the look on your face whenever I mentioned Ben. I don't know how you thought you could keep it a secret from me. Being a lawyer, I can find out just about anything about anyone."

My chin began quivering and I was on the verge of tears, I thought I had covered my tracks with everything with Ben. But I did just leave him with my parents.

"I will admit that I didn't know about him until after you left, but before then I didn't have any need to dig into your parent's information while you were with me. But when I found out that I had a son that you hid from me, I was shocked and then appalled. It didn't take much time for me to figure out that you had changed your name. Sheridan," he glanced back up through the mirror to where I could see the pity in his eyes, "did you not think I couldn't find you? You changed your last name from Meinshein to Nichols? At least next time change your first name as well to make it a little more challenging for me. I just had to bide my time until the right moment to come get you. Of course, you were always around Mike Jameson and by looking through his personal history, I could tell that he was a ticking time bomb that I really didn't have the patience to deal with. So I waited, weeks turned to months, then once you brought the boy here and Jameson was no longer coming around I knew it was now my time. But you began hanging out with someone new, my initial thought was that you were quite the little slut, but then I checked Deputy Ethan Bradley out and that boy is as queer as they get."

I didn't want to hear him slandering the people that I cared most about, but I really didn't have any other option. I should have just taken Ben with me in the beginning and ran off to Mexico, where we would've been completely out of sight. To think that I could've left him in harm's way by leaving him with my parents almost made me physically ill. I could feel my breakfast wanting to make a reappearance, but I had to quickly swallow it down. I knew Pate and the one thing that he absolutely hated was a mess. That would probably earn me the beating of a lifetime and then I would be forced to clean it up.

On second thought...I tried to quickly formulate my plan. I didn't know if it would work, but I had to take any chance that I could at this point.

I thought of him hurting my friends and loved ones and the sickness feeling was overwhelming once again that I just let it happen. I proceeded to throw up all over his floorboard.

"What the fuck?" Pate screamed before he craned his neck to see what just took place in his backseat. "God dammit, Sheridan." I knew his tolerance for puke was nonexistent. I felt him take a sharp turn to where I was sliding towards the door, my head first. I could just see my purse on the floor in front of me, but I had no absolute way to reach it with my hands secured behind my back. And if he wanted me to clean up the mess, he would have to let me go...

He threw the car into park before he peeled himself out of the seat. I saw his menacing face right before he jerked the backdoor open, covering his face with his free suit clad arm, to try and deter the smell. He had a weak stomach, so I knew that the stench was getting to him. I was really surprised he wasn't retching.

I felt his cold, clammy hand on my bare calf before he drug me out. He luckily moved his hand from my leg to one of my arms so I could stand up. But the feeling of being on my own two feet didn't last long before he shoved me to the ground.

"You dumb bitch!" he spat out in my general direction. "I really don't know why I made such an effort to find you when you are absolutely useless."

"Why did you then?" I yelled out before I had a chance to think better of it. His glare became more threatening and I knew that I had done it. I had messed with a sleeping bear and now he was up and ready to attack.

He lifted me up to where I thought he was going to put me back on my feet, but he kept lifting me to where I was even with his face, my feet dangling barely reaching the ground from my tiptoes.

"Because you are *mine*, Sheridan! *Mine!*" I smelled the lingering effects of tequila and tried to turn my face to where I wouldn't directly feel the harshness of his words or his breath, but he shook me until I looked back at him.

My body slammed against his car, my face leaning on the hot metal of the roof before he bent down to retrieve something from the center console. Pate made sure to yank at the zip ties to make them dig into my wrists before he used something to clip it off. I instantly moved my hands to the front of my body which was still pushed up against his car.

He jerked me around to where I was now facing him and my back was now forced against the car. "You will clean this mess up," he pointed to the back floor board. I guess I didn't make the confirmation that he was waiting for, because I was so relieved for my hands to be free so I could possibly carry out my plan. So with the same hand that he was pointing with, he proceeded to backhand me across my face. I raised my hand to my cheek where the after effects of the slap stung my face. I felt a wetness form in the corner of my mouth and brought my hand away to see that he drew blood. This man had drawn blood for the last fucking time.

But he wasn't finished, holding onto me on my shoulder with one hand he reared his other back and punched me in the stomach, knocking my breath clean out of me.

Grasping my stomach, I pulled away from his hold and began coughing and trying to catch my breath, taking deep gasps.

"That's so you don't try anything. You will clean up your mess that you made with your own clothing, then we will go on about our merry way." He turned on his heel and walked a few feet away from me.

I finally caught my breath enough to where I could stand upright once again, but not without pain. I was surprised that Pate took it so easy on me, but then again after I get his precious car cleaned up that might be a different story.

My hair had now come out of my twist that was secured on my neck due to his unnecessary roughness, but everything to Pate was justified.

Before I slid back into the backseat of his car, I looked around the vacant parking lot to see if I could tell where we were. Nothing caught my eye because there was literally nothing around. We must have been on the outskirts of Brown County. No trees or shrubbery in sight so my first idea of making a run for it was nixed. There was no place for me to run to so it would have made it less than difficult for Pate to quickly catch up with me especially since I would've been on foot and him in a car.

I untied my apron from around my waist so I could begin cleaning up the mess, no telling how long he would give me. I very carefully glanced his way to only find him on his cell phone. Good, so he wasn't paying close attention to me.

I reached for my purse taking out my cell phone and first dialed Tessa's number. I couldn't hold the phone to my ear in case he turned to check on me, so I laid it in the seat and hoped that after waiting a few seconds she would have picked up.

I knew that I couldn't talk long or too much, so I kept it very brief and to the point. "Tessa, help me!" I said at almost a whisper then hung up the call. I didn't know if anything would come of it, but at least someone would know that I was in trouble.

Sliding my phone back into my purse, the knife that I took from The Diner was staring me back in the face. I looked back to make sure Pate was still on the phone, in which he was. I contemplated if I wanted to be that person, to take matters into my own hands. I was fearful for my life and for my son's life. It would be worth it in the end to not have to constantly live in fear or worry about Pate lurking in the shadows for his perfect chance.

Who knew what would happen to me if I didn't take this chance. I had made my decision, I just hoped that it would be the right one.

I finished cleaning what I could of my sickness and slid back out of the car the same way I came in. I slowly and meticulously moved towards Pate, who still had his back to me and his phone to his ear. He never could live without his phone being attached to his hand and at this time I was purely thankful for it.

I pulled the knife out of the pocket to my uniform dress and I continued creeping as quietly as I could. I prayed that he wouldn't take this moment to turn around and check on me, if so I would have to react much more quickly than I intended to.

I dug deep down and tried to remember all the times Pate hurt me, either by forcing me to have sex with him or literally beating me. I brought all of those feelings that I felt and what I was going through to the surface and went with it.

I wasn't going to be the victim anymore. If there was any one thing that I had learned from my time being with Mike and being away from Pate, it's that I was brave. I was a brave woman fighting for her freedom and to keep myself, but most importantly my son safe.

Drawing the knife up, I was ready to strike, but at the very last moment Pate started turning around. But he had no idea that I was right behind him, ready for that element of surprise.

CHAPTER 21

Mike

It had already been one hell of a shift and I finally had my first moment of the day to rest. I took what time I could to lay outstretched on my cot with my arms folded behind my head just looking at the ceiling. I had never really noticed all the cracks that were apparent, but then again this building was pretty old.

In Brown County, all of the emergency services were housed in one building in a centralized location in town. That meant that the Sheriff and Fire Departments, the Ambulatory services and dispatch were altogether. It made sense to have it together and being each service had different floors for their rec rooms and cots, it worked out. I hardly ever had to deal with Ethan Bradley and when I did I just made sure to keep my distance.

Still staring at the ceiling, I thought back over the last few weeks without Sheridan in my life. It was back to being dull and lifeless as it was before she came into my life. I hadn't even really seen her since that night at Emmy Lou's. I had heard through Brock that Ben was now living with her and that his wife and mother had been taking turns watching him.

It was hard to hear Brock go on and on about how well Ben and Blake played together. Being so close in age, I supposed that it was good that they each had someone to play with.

I was happy for Sheridan even if the feeling of jealousy outweighed that happiness. Don't get me wrong, I was glad that she finally had her son with her, but it should be me with her and not Ethan.

The intercom came on and signaled that we had a call but that both ambulances were needed. *Great,* I thought to myself as I hopped up off of the cot, another bad wreck was the first thing that ran through my mind. I hustled down the stairs to the bay where the ambulances were kept and climbed in the passenger seat where Todd was already ready and waiting in the driver's seat.

"I guess it's bad enough that we need both buses, huh?" I asked Todd as I pulled the seatbelt across my lap and latched it securely.

"Yeah, but the location doesn't make sense. It's just outside of Brown County, where there is basically nothing left. Remember when they tore down those empty buildings a few years ago because of the squatters? That's where it is. There is really only empty parking lots."

As we bypassed the town, I was beginning to feel more and more uneasy about all of this. Something was niggling in the back of my mind that I wasn't going to like what was going on.

My phone rang on my hip and it was Sheriff Hennings so I didn't hesitate in answering it. Sometimes he called us ahead of time to relay what the situation entailed.

"Jameson," I answered into the phone.

"Mike, its Charlie. I just wanted to give you a heads up on the scene that you will be coming upon." I heard him take an audible swallow.

"It's Sheridan…"

A million different thoughts raced through my mind and in the end every single one had the same outcome. I couldn't lose her. I had already lost Hannah, I couldn't lose Sheridan too.

"Todd, you've gotta step on it. It's Sheridan, you've gotta *move!*"

There was no way in hell that it would take us those twelve minutes to get to her. Even with it being a little farther than the runs that we were used to, there was no way in hell that I would let it take us that long.

I had my medical kit ready and waiting on my lap and my seatbelt unbuckled before Todd skidded the bus to a stop in front of the scene.

Both of the Sheriff's Department vehicles were in attendance, which included Charlie's Camaro since he wouldn't use the standard issued vehicle that was provided to him.

The other ambulance came up moments behind us as they followed the entire way, even speeding up when we did.

Since I was the head paramedic on duty I directed them to the other victim and I ran straight to Sheridan.

Of course Deputy Bradley was in my way and I didn't hold my displeasure of him being so close to her.

"Back up Bradley so I can assess the situation." I tried to keep it professional but really I just wanted him away from her.

He quickly moved out of my view and I saw Sheridan sitting up on the asphalt with tears streaming down her face, wielding a cloth covering her arm.

She held her arm close to her body, so when I crouched down to her level and reached out for it the first thing she did was look at me with those piercing green eyes and then the dam broke loose letting the obvious tears she had been holding back run free.

Before I took a look at her arm, I had to breathe a sigh of

relief. She was here, she was breathing. I knew she would be alright.

I had to hold myself back from enveloping her in my embrace. I needed to remember that she wasn't mine.

I gently took the cloth off of the wound and began looking at the injury. My head snapped up to her, "This is a knife wound." I could tell by the depth and the placement of the cut that it was from a knife.

I wanted to get up to see who the other person was, but I couldn't be away from Sheridan. Although I had my suspicions, Sheridan confirmed them for me just a few moments later.

"Mike, I'm alright." The worried expression on her face told me that she wanted to get through to me that she was indeed fine. "It was Pate," she insecurely lowered her head to where she was looking at the ground.

My blood began to boil and I had to control my urge to go over there and finish off Pate myself. But there was no need to.

"He's dead." Those two words were the next to escape through her lips and she almost sounded as relieved as I immediately felt.

I couldn't hide the smile that was starting to form on my mouth as I asked her, "Did you..."

She shook her head, "no," quickly banishing that notion from my thoughts. It didn't really matter at the time, she was safe and she was right in front of me.

Deputy Bradley crouched down beside us but was ignoring me as he spoke only to her, "We are going to have to get your statement."

"Not in my bus you aren't. She has to get to the hospital for stitches and to make sure that no tendons were injured. You want a statement on the way to the hospital, you get Charlie to do it." Quickly chiming in, whether my opinion was warranted or not. It was *my* watch, *my* bus, he followed *my* rules.

He let out another sigh of displeasure as he returned to his full height, "Jameson, we need to talk...*now!*"

"Later, I'm busy." I was working on wrapping up her arm so it would stop the bleeding so she could take the trip to the hospital, with me.

"Fine, you don't want to listen to me Sheridan you can burst his bubble on the way."

She creased her brow and quickly tried to shake off his request, but it was too late, Ethan had already walked away.

I didn't want to try to think of what she would say that would burst my bubble so I tried focusing on getting her arm in transporting condition.

Getting to my feet, I helped Sheridan up and noticed she was limping, I didn't even take a look at the rest of her. I tried to stop her on the way to the ambulance, but she refused and climbed in sitting on the stretcher still holding her arm in front of her.

She wouldn't even look at me now. But her defiance let me peruse the rest of her body and I saw that she had some cuts and abrasions on her left knee. It even looked to the extent of a few rocks had embedded their way into her skin.

Whatever happened out there she didn't go down without a fight. I couldn't have been more proud of her.

Right before Todd closed the back doors to the bus, Charlie quickly slipped inside complete with his statement clipboard.

So it looked as if we were going to get to the bottom of what happened on the way.

Since Sheridan's injuries weren't life threatening we didn't have to speed or turn on the sirens, so we had plenty of time during our ride.

"So, Sheridan, I'm going to tell you what I know, then I want you to fill in the gaps." Sheriff Hennings started.

He was in complete professional mode, but the sadness lurking behind his eyes showed to me that he cared above and beyond his line of duty.

"I tell you what, I feel like I've been on a constant adrenaline rush ever since I received the call from Tessa." He sat back slumping in his seat, trying to relax a bit.

I didn't understand what he meant, why would Tessa know anything?

"Ok, here is what I know. Tessa called me directly stating that she got a call from you on your cellphone and all you said was 'Help Me.' She called me right after you hung up the line. I'll have to commend her for her quick work and she did so without a quirky comment too." He grinned which in turn made Sheridan grin. It was then I noticed the little cut near the crease of her mouth. *That bastard.*

"She told me that you were supposed to be at work so that was my first call. When Archie told me that you had left sometime earlier and he thought, you seemed a little strange but just shrugged it off. I'm sure he'll ream your ass later for not saying anything to him." Then he gave her a little wink. "Anyways, I called my FBI contact and good friend Hunter Severin to see if he could trace your cell phone. Smart thinking for you to keep it on so it could be traced and for not getting caught using it. Your bravery was the key to me finding you." Elation soared deep within my chest, she was so brave for what she went through.

"But I'm not brave. I thought I was. But in the end I couldn't kill him. I had changed in a way to where I knew that I wasn't going to go down without a fight as I had in the past, but I also couldn't bring myself to his level. I'm not a bad person and I wasn't going to have that on my conscious. But if you hadn't shown up when you did Charlie, then I don't know what would've happened. Maybe something in me would've snapped and I would've went ahead with it, but now I'll never know. But I'll also never have to live my life in fear ever again." Sheridan went on to tell us exactly what all happened, from her throwing up in his car because she knew he wouldn't be able to stand it so he would cut her free. He fucking tied her up using zip ties as if she were an animal. The way I was feeling if he weren't dead, I would've finished the job myself.

Then she proceeded to tell us that how she had the knife out that she took from The Diner and he ended up turning around so she quickly stabbed him in the back right where his kidney was located.

He ended up redeeming himself and got her to the ground and the knife out of her grasp, cutting her arm during the scuffle. Evidently he was in the process of getting ready to stab her again when Charlie arrived and shot him then and there on the spot.

I couldn't contain myself anymore, I grabbed her cheeks and looked into her eyes and then went in for the kiss. If Ethan wanted to kill me later, then he and I would hash it out then. But for now I wanted to kiss the woman who I was madly in love with because she did an amazing job getting herself out of a terribly horrifying situation.

I gently pressed my lips to hers, careful of the cut that was in the corner. It didn't take her long before she relaxed into me and I was able to sweep my tongue into her mouth which was promptly met with hers. We danced that same song and dance, our mouths intertwining like they did every other time before, so perfectly together.

Although I wouldn't regret this kiss, ever, I was the first to break free. I rested my forehead against hers as I muttered. "I'm sorry and I'll deal with Ethan later, but I had to kiss you. But the thing is you kissed me back…" She actually kissed me back. Hope spread throughout my chest and then I hoped that she wouldn't end up slapping me for what I had done.

"Mike has anyone ever told you that you jump to conclusions?"

"My dad did just a few weeks ago actually, why?" I was

still reeling from that kiss that my mind hadn't really caught up to my mouth.

"Ethan and I aren't together. He was there for me when I needed a friend. He's actually gay."

I reared my head back, shocked after hearing of this turn of events. I looked over to Charlie, actually having forgotten that he was there, but with a confused expression and he nodded affirming what she just said.

"Huh, I never knew he was gay."

"Well, no one around here really ever knew that you were married before now do they?"

Well except now for Charlie, I thought. I looked over to him and did a small shake of my head urging him to let it go.

"Not everybody airs out their business. I wouldn't have ever told you if Ethan hadn't just told me that it was ok to 'burst your bubble.' So, yes, I did kiss you back and I would do it again. But first I need to apologize." She took a second to glance at her wrapped up injured arm before returning her gaze to me. "I need to apologize to you for keeping you in the dark about Benjamin and although I had my reasons I should've trusted you with my sons life the way that I trusted you with mine. But in the end I knew the outcome would've been the same, I was just prolonging the inevitable. And even though I so desperately tried to not fall in love with you, it didn't work."

I opened my mouth and then shut it again trying to comprehend all of what she just said.

"You love me?" I asked incredulously. She had friend zoned me, then left my bed after we made love, and now she says that she loves me?

"I've loved you all along, Mike. I really tried not to because I knew your views on children and well Ben and I are a package deal. But I couldn't stop loving you even if I tried."

A single tear slipped down her cheek and I made quick work to wipe it away with my thumb as I caressed her cheek.

"I love you too, Sheridan."

"I know. You said it in your sleep that night. That's when I knew that I had to start pulling back. I couldn't crush you again with things you didn't know about."

I thought I had been dreaming that but to know that she did indeed love me well, it was a start. I didn't hesitate in diving in for her lips once again, tenderly kissing her and expressing how much I've missed her since she'd been gone.

"Ahem…" I faintly heard from the other end of the ambulance, but I was too into this kiss with the love of my life to bother stopping now.

"Mike, Sheridan, we are at the hospital." Charlie said.

I reluctantly broke apart the same time she did to realize that Charlie and Todd were both standing outside of the ambulance with the doors wide open.

Charlie rolled his eyes before he started leaving and I could hear him say, "I felt like I was living in a fucking soap opera for the last twenty minutes. My God, do they need to get a room."

I couldn't agree with him more but first we had to get Sheridan's arm and leg checked out.

Luckily the hospital wasn't busy at all and they were able to take a look at her arm and stitch her up within a few minutes and clean out the cuts on her leg and within an hour she had been discharged. And I only had to be told to quit hovering over her one time. I consider that a win because I wasn't going to let her out of my sight for a second.

Todd and Charlie had long gone with the ambulance leaving me behind without transportation. That was alright though because I was with Sheridan and she was all I needed at the moment.

After catching a ride back to the Station, I found that Todd had left me to clean the ambulance and get it set up for the next run. I had an incentive to get it done faster, I was just lucky that she decided to stick by me.

"Let me hurry up and get this cleaned up then I'll take you to your car, ok?"

I didn't really know what was going to happen from here on out, but I knew that I didn't want Sheridan to slip through my fingers again.

Once I had restocked the bus and put everything back in place, I sat down beside Sheridan who was resting on the back bumper of the ambulance, swinging her legs like a little kid.

"What are you thinking about?" I asked as I gently bumped her shoulder with mine.

She hesitantly shrugged her shoulders then brought her hands in her lap and began picking at her nails. I wasn't sure if she was trying to avoid my question until she finally spoke up.

She turned her head to the side to where she could look directly into my eyes, "Where do we go from here Mike?"

I hopped up from off of the bumper and began walking around aimlessly. Almost to the point where I was pacing back and forth.

I could tell that she wasn't going to sugar coat things, especially with having her son around. So if I wanted her I had to be completely all in.

I already knew that both of our hearts were on the line, but I didn't know if I had the actual strength within me to father another child.

Hope was reflected back at me from Sheridan's expression, she knew what she wanted. For her, her life would be complete with the three of us being together.

Two different options were staring me in the face and I hoped like hell that the decision I made would be the right one.

CHAPTER 22

Sheridan

I felt like I've held my breath for so long that I was going to end up passing out waiting for Mike's answer. Breathing wouldn't become easy again until he told me what he wanted and even then it may be hard.

My swinging legs had ceased their movement and I was beginning to lose feeling in my fingers from digging them over the side of the bumper. Not even to mention the constant throbbing in my arm from the knife wound.

My nightmare was officially over, Ben and I could live our lives in peace. Our family would be absolutely complete once Mike revealed his decision. I didn't want to feel like he was being faced with an ultimatum but in a way he was and I felt horrible for that.

But for me it was all or nothing. I was a packaged deal now. I had faith in him that he could become a father again and he would be amazing at it, because he was an amazing man.

An eternity passed again and I had to resume my breathing but that didn't mean that my violation of the bumper of the ambulance would stop any time soon. I was really surprised that my nails hadn't started ripping clean from the nail beds.

Finally, after I had almost given up hope, Mike stopped his pacing and stood directly in front of me. The way he was placed if he made the wrong decision I could easily swing my leg again and hit him square in the nuts, which would make me feel a teensy bit better if he told me he was done.

"Don't think that I can't tell what you are thinking. And you better get all violent thoughts out of your mind." He said with a smirk.

"Well, if you wouldn't take so long and either put me out of my misery or make me the happiest woman. The suspense is *killing* me." I said in a silly tone then quickly realized that I could've used a better choice of words and snapped my mouth shut.

Hmm… He seemed to mull over his decision once again before he solemnly said, "You and that smart mouth of yours... You'll have to give me some time for Ben and me to get used to each other. I'm not going to say that it'll be easy for me to let another child into my heart, but for you, for us…I am one hundred percent absolutely all in. I'll do whatever it takes to be with you Sheridan."

I didn't let him get in another word before I jumped onto him circling my arms and legs behind his back. It took him a moment before he regained his bearings after I forced him a few steps back.

Our lips met and I was first to slip my tongue into his waiting mouth. I would never get tired of kissing these lips and I would never get tired of loving this man.

Mike began walking forward and then I felt my back hit up against a cold, flat surface. I broke free to find that he had me pushed up against the back of the ambulance.

"We are far enough out of sight, if you'll be quiet, I'll be quick."

It took me a moment to realize that he was going to take me right here in the bay where the ambulances were parked.

My eyes grew wide and before I could say a word about it, he had set me down on my feet and bent down to slip my panties down my legs and stuffed them into his pocket.

He looked back up to me with a smile on his face and gave me a wink. "I've always wanted to do that," he said referring to putting my discarded panties into his work pants. Then he proceeded to unbuckle his belt and unfasten those same navy blue work pants pulling them down to free his impressive erection.

"You'll have to hold onto me, sweetheart."

I wrapped my legs around his waist once again as he cradled me under my ass slipping his erection deep within my core until he was completely seated.

I had never done anything as remotely as spontaneous or even in public for that matter.

"What if you get a call?"

"You worry too much, live a little," he whispered in between kissing my collarbone.

Worrying was my forte, it was what I did. But in this direction and me being in my uniform, I was covered more than he was. I had to start giggling at the first thing someone would see if they caught us.

"Oh, sweetheart, you've gotta stop giggling. That makes you clamp around my dick even more. Don't get me wrong it feels amazing, but this will be over entirely too soon if you continue." I didn't know if I would ever get used to him being so forward and so crass. "What was so funny anyways?" he added in.

"I was just thinking that in this position if someone were to walk in here and see us, the first thing they would see would be your ass." I couldn't help it, but I giggled again.

"What did I tell you about doing that?" he said in a joking

manner as he pressed his forehead up against mine. "Why do you think I put us like this? I wouldn't ever put you in a position to where someone else could see. No one else can see your goods, only me."

He continued pumping into me and I felt myself move closer and closer to the edge almost ready to tip into the pool of ecstasy but I wanted to hold off until he was ready.

"You'll have to hurry, baby. I'm so close, but I want to wait for you," my breathing was beginning to get more labored so it came out in a breathless whisper.

"I'm almost there." Our eyes locked once again and I could see all of his emotions and feels in the depths of those hazel irises. "I love you so much, Sheridan."

"I love you too, Mike." And we both catapulted over the edge into extreme bliss.

Before Mike, I didn't ever think that I would get the chance to live a life full of happiness. Now there were so many possibilities and I know that he would support me every step of the way. And I knew it would take time, but now Benjamin would have a mother and a father that he could look up to and never have to be afraid.

I prayed to God wanting something more and he sent me to Brown County where I met my love. Mike ultimately saved my life in more ways than one and for that I will forever be grateful.

Epilogue

Mike

Three Months Later

It's amazing how quickly things could change within three months…

Sheridan and Ben now lived with me which was an adjustment at first, but things seemed to be going well. It's only been for about a month since the lease was up on Maggie's apartment and since Sheridan was subletting she didn't have to renew it if she didn't want to.

It took some convincing on my part to get them to move in, but I think it has been the best decision.

The guest room has now been converted into a bedroom for Benjamin and true to little boy fashion he chose the *Cars* theme.

Meeting Ben officially for the first time had been an experience in and of itself. I thought it would be nice if we all took a trip to the Atlanta Zoo, to where we could be on more neutral territory. He didn't hesitate to kick me in the shin for being mean to his mommy at the hospital but by the time we were leaving he was asking me to bend down to his level so he could give me a kiss.

It caught me off guard and I'll admit stung a little when he went to give me an Eskimo kiss. That was Hannah and mine's special kiss and it just didn't seem right for me to do it to anyone else. That type of kiss wasn't very common so it surprised me that was the only way he gave kisses.

I didn't want to hurt his feelings, but he ended up alright with just a high five.

Not long after we started bonding my heart opened up for him. He was such a sweet and funny little guy that it was hard not to love him.

The way he would want to wrestle and then have to stop to readjust his little glasses. He was the complete opposite of my princess so it made it a little easier to move forward.

Getting off of shift, I couldn't wait to get home. I hadn't spent much time at the shop these days because my life was fulfilled just being at home with my family. And although Sheridan and I weren't married yet, someday it would happen but for now we were all content adjusting to everyday life.

I pulled into the driveway and parked right beside Sheridan's Monte Carlo. She absolutely loved that car and it warmed my heart that I was a part of making it safe for her.

Walking up the front porch I immediately heard music coming from inside the house. A smile automatically appeared on my face as I entered in through the front door.

Sadie didn't even greet me at the door like she used to, she was always otherwise occupied with Ben. They had become the best of friends and I was glad that Sadie Belle had someone younger to keep her on her toes a little more.

I leaned against the doorframe and crossed my arms in front of my chest in between the entryway and the living room and just watched the scene unfold before me.

Sheridan had quit The Diner after much apprehension on her part. She didn't want any ill feelings between her and Wanda and Archie, but she needn't have worried about that. Archie said that he was fine with her decision as long as we came for breakfast every Sunday and we had kept up on that promise.

Now Sheridan taught piano out of our home. She uses Ethan's Great Aunt Edna's upright piano and she has several students under her teaching now. She knew with her hands that she would never be able to complete Juilliard and fulfill her dream of performing so this was the next best thing for her.

Currently, she was in the middle of Grady and Emmalynne's son Tucker's lesson and apparently he was performing his rendition of "Mary Had A Little Lamb," or something that came close to that.

Sheridan and Ben were up dancing around to the sounds being made from the piano and from the looks of Sheridan's quirky and awkward movements she had been taking dancing tips from Tessa again.

I couldn't help the laugh that erupted from deep within my belly at the sight of them having a blast.

Finally, Sheridan had taken her spot back next to Tucker on the piano bench and began teaching him some other notes.

Ben resumed his playing on the middle of the floor with his matchbox cars and they still weren't even aware that I was home. It gave me a moment to look all around me.

Pictures of Ben and the three of us together were hanging on the wall. Even several pictures of Hannah had made their way to be showcased against the tan paint in my living room. Her pictures fit right in, like they belonged there. Sheridan surprised me with them one day and said they were where they supposed to be. I teared up, but it was because Sheridan was right, Hannah was right where she was supposed to be, next to her brother Ben.

I never thought that, after Erin, I would let another woman into my heart, but I have come completely full circle in life. I've learned that I could love a child again and it wasn't hindering my love for my little girl in any way.

Sometimes the best way to honor the life of someone you lost was to save another. I'll continue to save lives every day, but the biggest life that I've saved was not only Sheridan's but mine as well. I wasn't alone in that part, Sheridan was very much an active participant. But I ultimately made the decision to take a chance on a new love and a new family and I will never ever look back.

I pushed myself off of the doorframe and walked over to stand directly behind Sheridan and bent down to where I could wrap my arms around her and gave her a kiss on her neck.

She immediately placed her hands on my forearms and then turned around to look up at me smiling.

"Hey babe, I didn't hear you come in. Is everything alright?"

I couldn't contain my grin as both sides of my mouth tipped up, because everything was finally alright. "Yeah, everything is just perfect."

About the Author

I currently reside in Southern Indiana with my husband and two daughters. I spent most of my life trying to get out of Indiana, then spent four years trying to get back in, once my husband enlisted in the US Army and we were stationed at Fort Hood, Texas.

I am a stay at home mom and wouldn't have it any other way. Even though most of my time is spent transporting my girls to their various sports activities or running them back and forth to school, it is a blessing just to be with them each and every day.

I am a concert and road trip junkie! I love the thrill of seeing my favorite bands live, and just having fun on the open road.

My kindle has become like an extra appendage, as it is never far from my side. I became obsessed with books a little more than a year and a half ago and wished I had gotten into them much sooner!! My love of reading is what sparked my passion for writing, and now it's one of my favorite things that I do for myself.

CONTACT AMBER

On the web: Ambernationauthor.com

Follow on Twitter: @nation_amber

Facebook: Facebook.com/ambernationauthor

Email: ambernationauthor@gmail.com

Pinterest: http://www.pinterest.com/ber2885/

Other Books by Amber Nation

THE BROWN COUNTY SERIES

Not Alone – Grady and Emmalynne's Story

Runaway Love – Charlie and Maggie's Story
Now Available!

How to Save a Life – Mike and Sheridan's Story

Unconditionally – Toby's Story
Coming Soon!

Made in the USA
Charleston, SC
04 September 2014